TREASURE OF THE BLACK HILLS

TREASURE OF THE BLACK HILLS

JOHN B. PRESCOTT

CUTTING EDGE

ISBN-13: 978-1-954840-38-6

Published by
Cutting Edge Books
PO Box 8212
Calabasas, CA 91372
www.cuttingedgebooks.com

CHAPTER ONE

It was mid-afternoon when Ashley Merril came in sight of Matt Ross's place; and for the last mile or so across the scalded, barren bench, down through the snarl of half-dead mesquite trees that choked the dusty San Pedro bottoms, then up again to the bench on the yon side, he set his horse to running. Mindful of the day's pounding heat—that of every day this summer, in fact, and back before, too—he'd come along easy enough so far on his ride across from Huachuca Siding.

Now, though, with the buildings in view, he hurried. His horse would hardly suffer in the distance left; and anyway, his fear of finding Old Man Julius Harper not on hand and primed for more gold talk was greater. While Julius had been a come-and-go hand for Matt and other cowmen for some years, he was at heart a prospector, and lately, with the Valley burning up, he'd been talking up a mining party. It was talk so bright with treasure, so certain-sure of big bonanzas, that they might even be gone already. Ashley hadn't been there for a week.

But he needn't have worried. It was just like any other day these past two months when he'd gone to hear the talk and try to screw up his nerve to go with them. Julius Harper was there; so were Jack Campbell and Pat McGuire, hands of Matt's, too, and pretty well sold on Julius's idea. Coming up to the tangle of wire that did for a gate, he saw them all, along with Troy, Matt's son near Ashley's age, spraddled out in the tattery shade of a cottonwood tree down by the barn.

None of them looked like they had anything better to do, which wasn't surprising. No one had, these days.

Getting down, he led the calico horse through the gate. Down below they'd seen him now, but gave no sign. On his right, the square, plain house stood leaning on its shadow, the worn 'dobe blocks glinting straw, and the sun beating into the frazzle of shakes on the roof without mercy. In the heat and dust, there was no sound or motion until, as he neared, Troy hauled himself up and ambled into the barn. The others, though, still lay there like lizards in the swollen day.

Julius Harper was speaking on the drought; he always came edging at the mining talk, crabwise. On his chin, his beard fuzzed out in a fist of white, with his mouth a red gap that opened and closed with the words.

"A man can fight Indians," he was saying, as he might to a patriotic gathering. "Rustlers, too, and bad actors in town. But there's nothing on God's earth that he can do about a long-term dry."

Though he'd heard it all before, Ash was glad to be there for the beginning. They'd soon be asking his mind, and he didn't know it yet himself.

"Except to pray," Pat McGuire said, but in a way that seemed to make small of those who might. He was like that, Ash thought—a wiry, undersized man who seldom seemed to speak well of folks; except of Campbell, to whom he cottoned, but then not always of him either.

"Well, I'll own they're prayin' at Sulphur Spring," Julius said, squinting at the hot, milky sky. "Can't see much change yet though."

"You ain't yet give 'em time to dance the snakes," Jack Campbell said. "All they done so far is sing and shout."

Campbell laughed, and it occurred to Ashley that he liked his little joke now and again, providing he had a fitting butt for it. As a general thing, however, he was quieter than McGuire, as if his thoughts might best be kept private. He listened, though, with a dark eye turned on the speaker like a man who stores what he hears against future use. He was bigger than McGuire and, as the saying went, they ran together, though with Campbell ahead some. But beyond their living off the Rosses since hitting the Valley several months back, no one knew much about them. According to what Ashley heard, they were indifferent hands, but Matt was too soft-hearted to send them on in the midst of bad times.

"Hopi medicine," Julius said to that. "Ain't polite to laugh; but I frankly doubt they'll coax down more'n a squirt of bird pee."

As if the mere thought of the exhorting over at Sulphur Spring wearied him, Julius lay farther back against the log behind him.

"No, sir, a man can only sit and wait," he went on. "Unless," and here he held up while his eye slid around to each man.

"Unless he hunts gold," Campbell finished for him. "Come on, we've heard it all before; let's get at it."

"More meat than fat on that thought," Julius said, rousing of a sudden to aim an arm at Ash, who was pulling off his saddle. "How about it, boy? You're the one we're waiting on, and we can't wait forever."

Ash felt uneasy. Ordinarily, Old Man Harper's build-up went teasing on further, but not today. Time was too short now, and they wanted an answer. Still, he made a study of setting his saddle up on its bow and spreading the blanket on the cantle to dry.

"Well, I been thinking on it," he said, while he pulled a handful of hay from a butt standing near and began to wipe the sweaty hide.

"Nor of much else," Campbell said, "from the look of that horse."

"I only run a mile," Ash said. For all he was just a drifter, Campbell sometimes liked to lord it over a person. "A horse that can't do that, heat or no, ain't worth much."

"Can't hurt to find out," McGuire said in a grin at Campbell, "given you got a string to draw on as they die off."

Ash let that one go. It seemed to him that Pat spoke more for Campbell's ear, anyway, which he often did, though Campbell didn't always seem to hear. He reached for the olla that hung from the eave, and drank from it.

"Thinking's all right," Julius said, "but it's come time to act. If we're going, it better be quick. It's July now. We only got a few months till winter sets in."

Ash sat down against the log, angled so as to face the back of the house. Sounds from inside told of dishes being washed—Troy's sister Lilly, maybe.

Julius went on. "How about it, kid? You throwin' in?"

They'd decided, all right, Ash thought. And now they had to have his say because he could bring food. Still, he wanted more time.

"Be easier to say, could we tell ahead if it would pay or not."

"Godalmighty, what's worse than here? Been to the Siding, ain't you?"

Ash nodded, and Julius asked, "What's the prices?"

"Ten dollars prime."

Julius grinned. "A big fall from thirty, ain't it?"

Ash slid out his legs to full length, seeing on his old boots the dust of four years of drought, of falling prices, and in his mind's eye his folks' dismay at how a beef herd ten years in building could so swiftly dwindle to hide and bone.

"Well, I guess there ain't much going on here just now."

"You guess?" and Campbell grinned.

"Hold on there, Jack," Pat McGuire said. "You're forgetting that he's an owner's kid. He don't have a hand's view of things."

As if asking approval, McGuire glanced at Campbell, who laughed and slapped at his leg.

"Shoot, that slipped my mind. I guess it's bound to differ, at that. No, he ain't likely to feel the squeeze like us."

"You fellows ever try meeting a note at the bank?" Ash said. "You think owning stock's so easy these days, try it. The range is free."

"The dry lakes on Wilcox Flat are free to fish in, too," Pat said.

"Lord to God," Julius broke in, "a frying day like this, with all we got to talk about, and you pick nits."

Though the nit-picking gave him more time to think in, Ash was glad to leave it be. If he did decide to go, it would be bad to start off wrong with McGuire and Campbell. Maybe you couldn't blame them too much, anyway, for talking as they sometimes did, or for being anxious to get started. There'd been little work for hands lately, and a spell of riding the chuckwagon on owner's charity was hard on a man's pride. Almost anything was better. An owner might be broke, but still he had his own roof, his own beef to eat, and his own horses to ride.

In the little space of quiet that settled down, the men mopped at their brows and waved their hats slowly at their faces. Leaning back and letting his glance stray around, Ash saw Campbell's eye fill with distance, and what might be yearning; while McGuire, who watched him too, had a look that Ash could only think of as suspicion of where Campbell's far thoughts were ranging.

But then he could be wrong about both of them. After all, he hardly knew them, and he might better think kinder thoughts of them than that.

Just then Troy came from the barn, walked over and sat down beside Ashley.

"How, kid," he said. "You decided yet?"

"How, your ownself," Ash answered. "I been thinkin'."

"Shoo. I bet you ain't even asked your folks yet."

That was like Troy, Ashley thought—a piece of dry ground that soaked up all that fell on it. Sometimes it seemed to Ash that Troy was like a person searching for himself, and in the hunt took on from time to time the ways of whatever man or men that chanced to catch his fancy. These last few months with Campbell and McGuire living off Matt, he'd so shaped himself on their likes you questioned that he'd ever had a notion of his own. He had only a year on Ash, but he made it sound now like Ash was just learning to walk.

That he might guess that Ash's folks were still unknowing was like him, too; natural, likely. Their families had come to the Valley at the same time and they'd grown up together. They were friends of kid days and knew each other like brothers. Sometimes they fought so, too.

"They ain't spoke against it," Ash said, which was true, not yet having had the chance. "How 'bout you?"

"No trouble. You might say it pleased 'em. There's always the chance of finding something. And there's nothing doing here."

It was probably true. Letting Troy go would be a surefire way for Matt to get Campbell and McGuire and Julius off his back.

"That's what we been sayin'," Julius said. "Nothing doing here at all. Out there, a fortune's waiting. But we got to get started."

"You got to get off that pot, Merril," Campbell said.

"We can't go too thin," McGuire said, as if he, too, must speak since Campbell had. "Takes time to find another, if you ain't goin'."

Ashley let dust stream down through his fingers. It was wrong that they gang up on him. Mostly, he was fired up to go, but there were doubts that needed time to settle. There were his folks, too; he was an only child, and Pa was no spring chicken any more. It was easy for Campbell and McGuire to leave; they had nothing to lose, beyond steady rations. Neither had Julius, whose prime talk in all the years he'd worked around the Valley had been of what might be found in the hills beyond. And it was easy for Troy, too, with Matt so eager to lower the feed bill. But it was different with him.

Yet they had a right to know.

"Maybe I'd know quicker if you told where we'd go," he said, and thought: There, let Julius squirm awhile. Saving in a vague, general way, he never *had* said where. He was ready enough to tell about all manner of past prospects, of long-gone glory holes that hadn't panned out; but never of where he might like to try next.

Julius threw up his hands. "Well, now! Like I said about gold ..."

"It's where you find it," Ash said. "I know. But I ain't asking that. I'm asking where we mean to look for it."

Old Man Harper scrooched and hunched about on the ground.

"Why," he said, sliding his eye around, "about a month out." His spade of a beard hacked an arc that covered the whole northern horizon. "I figure that way's best."

Troy looked at Ash. "You could easier rope a mossy-horn five years in the brakes than pin Julius down to a direct answer."

"He wants one of us, though," Ash said.

The remark appealed to the others; maybe because the need for decision was on them.

"The kid's right," Campbell said. "You got to loosen up. I'm for it, but not to be tricked into chasing down your Lost Six-Shooter, or Lost Old Woman."

"Don't worry," Julius said, then added, "That don't mean they ain't out there, however, still waiting."

"Deal me out of Chiricahua country," McGuire said. "Pinal country, too. I ain't askin' to get skewered."

"We'll keep clear of them. Indians are elsewhere, though, too. That's just one of the chances."

"How about the Colorado?" Troy said. "The River?"

But Julius shook his head. "La Paz and Ehrenburg are dead, and the placers with 'em."

"Maybe the Bradshaws, then," Ash put in.

"Been pretty well covered by now," Julius said; he glanced at Ash. "You ain't so far off, though. She's north, all right."

Creaking and unsteady after sitting so long, he pushed himself to his feet and crossed to the olla. There was quiet while he held the clay pot to his mouth and wiped his beard on his sleeve afterward.

"But that's about all for now," he said. He drank again, and then said, as if the time had come for all to shoot plumb center and be square and honest, "It's only fair to say I can't guarantee no gold; but I can guarantee a place to look for it in. One that ain't been picked over and worked to death by others ahead of us."

CHAPTER TWO

Ashley let himself ease backward more, and for a space looked out across the baked ground beyond. The weight of the great dry crushed down upon all in sight. Nothing moved, and there was no sound either just now, saving the hum of flies feasting in the scatter of manure.

Coming right down to it, he thought, Julius hadn't had much of an answer, even now. A month away, and north; but no more. Except that it would be a place that no one else had heaped up with tailing piles before them, and so would be virgin ground. But then that was something; and maybe no more than you could hope for now in the eighties when a good deal of Arizona had long since passed through rocker boxes or stamp mills or concentrators.

And maybe no more than you could expect of Julius, either, he thought. For all it wasn't much, it was still more than he'd ever let out before; and in his mind, he likely felt he'd spread himself generous.

It made you want to laugh—just thinking of the rickety lean-to where Julius lived down in a mesquite thicket when not at work as a hand or prowling the hills, or of the handful of cows he ran and sold now and then at the Fort; sometimes mavericked, it was said. While meantime spinning yarns about famous diggings and making out that he could take you to a king's ransom—telling just enough to make you think there might be some truth in it. It pulled on you, all right.

But it was funny, too; and had it hung alone on the hope of finding gold, why, Ash guessed he wouldn't go. But there was more to it than that. Not that he'd decided yet, for all their pushing.

The talk had changed now. It was on supplies, and they were telling what they'd need to take, and what they might be able to get from the land as they traveled. Ashley listened with a part of his mind, while another ambled off on its own to dally with the chance to see new country, the weary hopeless feeling that a long dry gave you, and what you felt at eighteen that made you want to push out of wherever you were, and go, if only for the sake of going.

A fellow ought to go while he could. Soon enough a time could come when, like his pa, he'd be worn down in spirit and body to the point of seeking refuge in the Bible.

"I got a little powder cached away," Julius said. "Sealed her up in a mud-bank above run-off level. Ought to be good yet."

Pat McGuire asked about tools.

Julius said he had a few odds and ends of that kind. Troy thought he might scrounge something, too.

"Merril can fill out the rest, likely," Campbell said.

"Some owner has to," Pat said. "Hands never have such."

True enough, Troy agreed, as if he would agree to almost anything that Campbell and McGuire said.

"There's staples," Julius said. "Can't leave them to chance."

"Well, there again," Campbell said, "you got owner's doings. Seldom see a hand packing fifty pounds of flour from job to job."

"Hands don't have no money these days, neither," McGuire said.

Ash brought back the far-off part of his mind. He leaned around Troy to look at Pat.

"Some day you come over and count all our money," he said.

Pat's mouth sprang open like a trap, but he whined the words out, as a man asking favors will.

"You ne'en worry about us pulling our rightful share of the load," he said, and maybe more was coming, but Campbell cut him off, sounding as if Pat had said enough, and wrong, maybe, at that.

"We all got to help the best we can," he said. "You three drag the gear and staples; me and Pat'll keep the meat pot filled. Don't think you can live on flour and water."

"I ain't said we could," Ash told him, "but I figured we'd split the hunting; me and Troy, anyhow. Given I go along, that is."

"No need to," Campbell said as if it were all settled. Then he said, "Me and Pat are good shots," as if there were no question how they stood in that regard, and so made it natural that they should be free to range the hills and forests for game, while the rest concerned themselves with firewood and pack saddles and squaw work in camp.

When Lilly came out of the house with the bucket of rinse water, the talk slowed and for a space drew up, and then as she crossed over to the kitchen garden past the windmill and tank, it went on.

Ashley stood up. "That bucket reminds me," he said. "I guess my horse could take on some water now."

He'd been wondering how to go about it, and he guessed it passed. No one spoke, and only for a second did something stand in Campbell's eye, seeming to say that he saw through Ashley's remark. But Ash could be wrong, too. It might only be another of those moments when Jack's thoughts were yondering forward, or backward, toward better or other times. Or it might be nothing.

At the tank, so as to seem uncaring, he kept his back to Lilly. But he also stood no more than two yards down water of the pipe that dribbled out a thin trickle from the smaller tank above, fixed to the frame of the windmill.

It was from this pipe that Lilly hung her empty bucket when she brought it back from the garden plot.

"My, my, Ashley," she said, "how ever can you stand to leave the gold-hunters, even for a minute?"

Ashley made himself seem surprised to see her there next to him. Looking around, he saw her eyes filled with blue sky, and her hair yellow and bright in the sunlight.

"Why, hello, Lilly," he said; then went on, "I guess water stands ahead of gold, don't it?"

"Wouldn't know it from the way you've carried on this past month."

"Well, it does now," Ash said.

Lilly turned her head and watched the water run down from the pipe. She was younger than Ashley by two years, and only six months ago was still no more than a leggy, bothersome splinter of a girl. But she was different now in some way. She'd changed in that time, her body going strangely firm and slender in her shoddy old dress, her eyes alert to all about her, and so aware that all she felt and thought seemed to show in them. She was bothersome still, however—but in a manner that confused him, even annoyed him.

When she turned again, it was one of those times. "When do they plan to leave?" she asked.

"The sooner the better," Ash said, "according to Julius."

"Him," she said. "I'd bet he's only telling tales to pass the time of day. Pa says he could talk the handle off a well pump."

However much Julius liked to air his tongue, Ashley still felt moved to defend him. "Why," he said, "it seems to me that what a man says is what counts. Not how much. I'd say he knows plenty."

"If that's the case, then, why isn't he rich? He's forever telling of his gold mines. Where are they?"

Ashley wasn't so much aware of Lilly's newness any longer; she was getting to be more like her old self every minute. "Just because he ain't rolling in gold don't mean he's ignorant."

"Seems to point that way." Lilly looked into her bucket again. Then, while her head was turned yet, she said, "I don't guess you'll be going along though, will you, Ash?"

From the sound of her voice, it was hard to tell how the question was meant. But he wasn't going to say that he hadn't yet decided. She might take it as agreement with her notions on Julius.

So he said, "Well, I sure don't know why I shouldn't."

"Your ma and pa will have a few reasons why not."

In the way that she had known him so long, and so felt free to poke among his private doings, she was like Troy. Sometimes he felt about her as he felt about Troy, too.

"How do you figure that out? Troy's going, ain't he?"

"With more to feed, it's different here. He's older'n you, too."

There was no confusion in how she bothered him now. Few quarrels in the past had failed to touch on his being younger than Troy.

"You been saying that for ten years," he said. "You ought to know I'll never catch up. That don't mean I'm any kid, though, like you say."

"Now, Ashley, don't take on," Lilly said.

"I ain't," he said, though he knew he was and that her saying so made him take on more. "But I've got the same right to go as Troy."

"I didn't say you hadn't the right," Lilly told him, and she turned again to the bucket, near filled now, and with her head tipped, Ash was made aware of the line of her neck and its soft curve at her shoulder. The tip of a pink ear peeped through her hair.

Somehow, his being aware of that grace and line was at the middle of his feelings. Just to recognize it made him boil over. "And it ain't your business, anyhow!" he flared up, half in a shout.

As if jerked, Lilly turned again, and there came and went in her eyes what might have been hurt—but too quickly to be sure of. Not speaking yet, she took the bucket down from the pipe; then, going off, she tossed him a glance and said; "I guess you're right, Ash; it ain't my business, at that."

Ash stood a moment watching her go; her walk was like her softly curving neck, and all else strange and new about her, making him mad all over again. Then, when he turned away, he saw the others watching him—speculating. Well, he didn't care if they *had* heard; he only cared that they know he was his own man. He guessed that Lilly, an altogether brat, knew it now. It wouldn't do no harm if they knew it, too.

Behind him, the calico's belly gurgled on its fill of water. No doubt he'd let it drink too long, and would be lucky to reach home without trouble.

CHAPTER THREE

It would be near midnight, Ashley thought, with some hours yet remaining before time to roll out. But he knew he wouldn't sleep any tonight, the way his mind ranged back and forth between gold country and home, where he now lay waiting for things to begin.

One minute his thoughts would be dwelling on gold wires that harbored in rose quartz; in the next, his pa would be there talking grim and somber about duty and denial.

They'd always been religious people, but the last few years had seen Pa take to Bible reading more and more. The longer the dry, the more time he spent with it, trying to find reasons and explanations for calves that starved for want of milk, for cows that ran about wild-eyed until they fell, and for water that filled the river bed only in a sudden, churning run-off of rain that fell too far away to know where. And in the end seeing it as a test.

That's right: and with his elbows on the table and his long face both grim and sad above his folded hands, you could see him facing that test. Nobody had a right to think that life should be an everlasting flow of milk and honey, without a trial now and then. No indeed. Adam and Eve fixed that. A man could only face what came without complaining and whining until it let up. And running off on a wild-goose chase for gold, meantime, wouldn't help things.

Though he hadn't said it right out, it was plain to Ash that Pa was drawn to look on that as a sign of weakness.

Ash was in bed in the dark of the small room that served partly as his bedroom, and partly as a catch-all kind of room off the kitchen. Outside in the brush and rock and cactus, the night things were stirring. With the sun's heat out of the bottoms, little sidewinders would be uncoiling in the sand to stalk deermice and kangaroo rats and other small creatures. Fist-size, burrowing owls would be sitting by their holes like stone statues, waiting for bugs and mice. Here and there a ring-tailed cat or kit fox would be hunting quail—though the want of cover this year had made nesting poor, and the unshielded eggs often fried before hatching. From somewhere he couldn't place, there came a soft, steady sound, as of a badger digging.

Rolling over, he looked around the dark room. On the packed 'dobe floor, the thin sliver of new moon had laid a patch of light. Beyond a few feet, and seen more by memory than clear sight, a sack containing a shirt or two, a few pair of socks, an old threadbare woolen jacket and spare jeans, hung from a nail in the wall. Also in the sack there was a Model 1861 percussion-cap Colt revolver with a broken sear, a little buckskin bag containing primers, ball, and paper cartridges, a belt knife with its handle bound in wire, a coil of fish line—if water enough to hold fish was ever found—and another small bag, a cloth one, that held coffee. In the corner, and unseen in the flood of dark, stood a still bigger sack, near filled with flour.

Of all gathered there against leaving, the flour sack stood biggest in meaning. Any way he looked upon it, that was pure sacrifice. All else could be put away in its chest, or on its shelf, or hook or nail, and the whole idea of going be forgotten, even now.

But not that flour sack. For into that, along with each grain that Ma had scraped together and hoarded for him, had also gone many a look of damp eye and shake of head, and from Pa many a snort and complaint about the cut in the biscuit ration. Every day of its standing in the kitchen, it swelled bigger, and every day, too, its presence put in Pa's mind more reasons why Ash should stay home where he belonged.

"Faith," he'd say. "You got to have faith that the Lord knows best. What if we *all* run off, every time things went bad?"

Ash couldn't answer that. For all it was beyond him why drought was best now, there was still no laughing at Pa's talk of faith. More than once in fifteen years in the Valley there'd been little else. Back in the Indian trouble, faith alone had seen them through the time they'd been burned out. Without that they might never have made a go of it.

Still, Ash couldn't believe that a few months' absence would make any difference one way or the other.

Again, Pa'd say, "I ain't sure it ain't a sin to leave now, Ash. Shows the Lord you don't think much of how He runs things."

Pa's God was jealous and demanding, and stood for no foolishness on doubtful matters. In a question where temptation cropped up, you'd better shy off.

Pa also had frowns for gold-hunting; money of that kind, chanced on and stolen from the earth—raped, you might say—was ill-gotten; tainted. The only honest kind grew from grass into beef, or from seed into a crop.

Then, reaching that point, it was only a step to Pat McGuire and Old Man Harper and Jack Campbell.

"Landless," he'd say, as if the one word told all. "Such kind won't lead you anywhere but into trouble. Troy don't surprise me, but it's beyond me why you're so taken with trailing after them."

"I don't aim to trail them," Ash said, and then he went on and tried to tell how he simply wanted to go, that he wasn't trailing anyone.

But there seemed no way for him to say what he felt, to say that no argument whatever held water now that he'd decided, and to say that Lilly, by laughing at him and making little of him, had cinched it. That all argument just made him more decided.

So he'd simply kept silent these past ten days or so and let Pa go on; until now, when he lay in bed with the hour of leaving soon to come, more set in his mind than ever, and ready to show them all.

Ash rolled over once more, thinking how he'd show them, how he'd come back richer than the king of Babylon—or anyhow, would learn to live his own life. But somewhere in the middle of his rolling over, his bones and muscles flattened out and relaxed, and the thought went on alone into a dream.

Over the bed, something hard and small clicked at the window. Down at the barn, the Merrils' old dog Shep cut loose, then grew quiet again, as he always did on learning it was friends about.

Still coming out of sleep, Ash lay quiet until the sound came at the window another time—a sure-enough stone, it was. "It's them!"

He sat up and swung his legs out, all in one motion. He reached for his jeans and hopped about on one foot getting into them. He stumbled into his boots, and made for the door that led outside.

A shape moved in the dark, came near and grew to be Troy. "Ash?"

"It's me."

"Bust your butt, boy; gold's awaitin' in them hills."

"Won't take me a minute," Ash said. "All out there, are you?"

"Yes, and ready to roll."

Ashley's eyes poked through the dark beyond Troy. Out on the trail that wound through the Valley, other shapes moved and stood still and moved again. In the still, early air, a wagon wheel creaked.

"We're all here," Troy said, as if to hurry things. "Pa come, too, this far, to say good-by. You want me to rig your horse?"

"All right," Ash said, while he buttoned his jeans. "I'll take my calico, I guess. There's a stock saddle hanging near the door." Then he stopped and thought again; Pa deserved consideration. "Better take the McClellan; the bridle's hanging with it. Don't mind Shep."

"I ain't scared of him," Troy said, going off.

Closing the door, Ash pulled on his shirt and stuffed the tails in. Then he took up his hat and the two sacks and went out into the main room. He'd hoped to get away unnoticed, without the wear and tear of good-bys, but he might better have hoped to fly.

Already, under the door of his folks' room, light flickered; then Ma came out with the lamp, her faded wrapper buttoned up to her neck.

"You can't go without breakfast, Ashley," she said and set the lamp on the table. She moved to the food box. "Not with all the miles ahead of you."

Even in the poor light of the lamp, her weight of sadness showed. But she moved surely, and with sure hands took from the box the plate of biscuits and rib of beef and jug of milk left from last evening. He knew it cost her to do it, and for a moment he was caught up in the memory of all the other times that she had done that. She lived so in the shadow of Pa and all he stood for, or against, that her readiness to send her menfolk out always with full stomachs, come night or day, or whatever weather, almost slipped by.

Until a day came when you went hungry—then you remembered quick enough.

The thought that such might be required for him to see clearly all she did to keep them going, to hold their ground, on a sudden took hold in his throat. So that it wouldn't show on his face, he made a big thing of setting down the bags just so beside the door.

When he straightened, Pa was there, standing in the bedroom door, looking half shy, as if minded now to make peace.

"You got all you need, Ashley?"

"I reckon," Ash said; still careful, though. For all of Pa's appearance, he might yet have a round left in the chamber.

He took a biscuit from the table. Eying the sacks, Pa looped his suspenders over his shoulders.

"You got socks and underwear, I expect." And when Ash nodded, Pa said, "You got the Book in there, too?"

"I figured it might get spoiled or something," Ash said, and thought, now it's coming—a last-ditch preachment on God.

But no preachment came. Pa just bobbed his head and said, "It's up to you, though we could spare it. I guess we know it better'n you."

Of course, he had to say something; but that was all, and Ash was still wondering when the sound of Troy and the calico reached them. Pa pulled open the door, and the small light of the lamp reached out.

Troy made good mornings, then said to Ash, "You set?"

"Just now coming," Ash said, downing the milk.

Pa turned from the door. "You might take the burro, if you like, Ashley. Save your horse to spread the load." Then his glance veered and hunted around the room, while Ash wondered if he'd seen the old McClellan, or if, now that the moment had come, it was just his way to put aside stubbornness. Whichever, the bigness of feeling that Ash felt surprised him.

"Why, thanks," he said, "thanks a heap."

"You go get it," Troy said, as if time might be saved, "and I'll take your horse up. Give me one of them sacks, too."

Handing one over, Ashley held the other, and put on his hat. Ma came from the stove, and now, finally, there were tears; tears and good-by and good luck and take care against cold and wet, and Pa's hand in his, and watch their hoofs, boy, and keep clear of loco weed.

Then he'd turned, and was going through the door past Troy, out across the barnyard in the early coolness, and in the barn taking down a lead rope and halter and kyack and getting the burro in from the corral, and letting it munch on a small bait of corn while he put on the rigging and tied down the sack of flour.

Going out and up the grade toward the trail, Shep came up behind him, whining, as if knowing that whatever was afoot would see him left out. Drawing up, Ash reached down and felt the long head and soft, pointed ears. Shep was part collie and part shepherd and the rest catch-as-catch-can, and a fine dog, though getting along now.

"No, dog, you stay here," Ashley said; but Shep whined again, moving closer, and his tongue, wet and rough on the top, came out and licked at Ashley's hand.

"Well, all right, but only to the road."

He straightened and moved on, toward the snort and stamp of horses, which had caught the scent of Shep, the burro and himself now. And in a moment he saw their heads turned and their ears raised and aimed his way. As he stopped, they dipped their heads to sniff and blow at Shep.

Ashley said, "Howdy," and was surprised to hear Lilly's voice among the replies. Troy hadn't said about her. Looking around, he made her out on the wagon seat, beside Matt, but not plain enough to tell anything. Well, she'd better watch her tongue, that was all.

"You must have took time to milk the cows," McGuire said.

"I come as quick as I could," Ash said.

Julius, his beard frosty with starshine, came over and ran his hands along the kyack and pack.

"Ain't too bad," he said. "We can straighten things come daylight."

"Troy's got a sack of mine," Ash said, but couldn't make him out.

"He's just coming up from the house," Matt Ross said.

All turned to look, and as Troy passed before a lighted window, Ashley wondered if Pa had held him there an extra minute, maybe telling Troy to look out for him. Even now, likely, Pa couldn't leave him be.

Then Troy was there, and they were ready to move. From the wagon, Matt reached down and each in turn took his hand, while in the dark, voices called, *adios,* good luck, see you in November, yes, hope you pan a million.

Ash was last, having lashed the other sack in place. As he shook Matt's hand, the wheels were already moving and the wagon making its circle in the road to start for home. Ash dropped from the step and crossed the trail, and when it passed him going straight he stood on Lilly's side. He put his hand up in a wave. The motion caught her eye, and in a move so swift and made so much of darkness that he scarcely saw it, she leaned down, and with her lips, brushed his cheek.

"Good-by, Ash," she said. "Don't be sore at me. I didn't mean no harm."

Ash was too surprised to answer, or to move, and could only stand with the imprint burning his face while the wagon moved off on the road south. A little at a time he was aware that Troy was speaking.

"You deef? Here, take this thing. Your pa wants you to have it."

For its weight, Ash nearly dropped what Troy gave him — Pa's 44-40 rifle, wrapped in oily rags and cased in its saddle scabbard. Wound about it was Pa's belt, stuffed with cool, smooth brass.

"Your pa said, do you need a weapon, you'll need more'n that old cross-bow you got in your war-bag."

"Thanks," Ash began, but stopped because no more would come. His throat closed it off, and an ache filled him.

Then, in some way, it all changed; Troy had lingered some time at the house. "What else did Pa say? I'll bet he said for you to keep an eye skinned out for me—didn't he?"

"So, what if he did? You ain't any Kit Carson."

Troy mounted and drew off, and Ashley stood in the road and looked at the house on the slope of the bench below. As he watched, the pale light grew dim, and then the window went blind and black. Pa would be in bed again now. No more sound came from the wagon where Lilly rode either.

It was trickery, that's what it was, he told himself; Lilly and Pa both, each in his own way still trying to play on his youngness, trying to make him feel small—now that he aimed to show them; or something like that. But the littleness and smallness and aloneness that he really did feel wouldn't let him be certain.

East, the Dragoons began to shape themselves against a gray band; but it was still dark, and stars winked overhead. Mounting up and letting loose a length of lead line for the burro, he was glad of that. At his age, a fellow who was fighting back tears needed privacy.

Two or three miles had gone by before Ashley looked around much. Maybe half an hour had passed and they'd ridden all the while in silence, as men will in darkness, as if the dark had set down something of its own quiet on them. Having started last, Ash still trailed; but it suited him for now, though the still air allowed the dust from up ahead to come back over him.

Then with full light, the changes of the new day's coming could be seen and felt and heard. The Dragoons stood sharp against the clear, liquid light that flowed orange and yellow from the east, each ragged point of rock seen as through glasses, and the trees, upon the ridges standing as separate slivers with the sky behind them, like bristles on a brush. The night creatures were going into their secret hiding places, and the day creatures were coming out. Off toward the bottoms somewhere, a quail called out, half laughing, half asking. A pair of mourning doves winged over the line of march, moving very fast and hoo-hooing to each other in their rising, falling, twisting flight. Doves always flew as if they thought each second was going to bring birdshot up.

Someone, Campbell or Troy, called out something, and now Ash was made aware of other sounds that had awakened with day; or maybe had been there all along but only now were heard. Even the movement of the pack animals seemed louder, or anyhow busier. The dark had seemed to quiet all but the dull setting of hoofs. But full light brought also to the ear the squeak of leather and clank of snaffle, the rumble and grunt of bellies and passing of wind.

The awareness of all this, now that the sun was edging up, brought the burro to mind. He turned and saw it there behind him, trudging along the way it had been, though seeming some closer by daylight.

Then, still looking, his eye was caught by a vague and shadowy motion in the brush. It was such a motion as an animal will make that stalks its quarry while deciding when to leap. It would be a coyote, he thought, though it was strange behavior for such. Then he thought it could even be some loafer wolf, or old male lion.

Still watching, he put his hand down for the rifle; but hardly had he touched it than he drew it back. As if knowing now that it had been seen, the animal quit the brush and stepped onto the road.

Ash swore, in anger first, then with pleasure. It was Shep, coming on the run, his red tongue lolling out, and his tail swinging.

CHAPTER FOUR

Old Man Harper threw his diamond-hitch, drew his knee from the horse's belly, and tucked the end of the line in against flopping. Even was there no chance of that, he'd have tucked it in anyway; he liked things orderly on the trail and in camp. He might let his shack in the bottoms get sprawled out, but that didn't count as it was only a place to mark time between grub-stakes.

His true life lay on the gold trail, and all concerning it was deserving and demanding of care and respect.

No doubt his views had been surprising to the others, though, he thought now as he raised his hand to set them on the third day's mileage. That first day, anyhow, nearly all of which had passed in trying to teach them how to load their packs so they'd ride proper—and untangling them when they didn't—how to throw a diamond-hitch, how to make and break camp without a storm of dirt and dust, how to space out when moving. Having been raised in the country, you'd think they'd already know; but as cattle people, too, and used to having the cook take on the little household chores at roundup, as well as tote their bedding and gear in a wagon, why, they didn't, of course.

Talk about ignorant! And somewhat sassy about it, too, when mistakes were pointed out; although that early morning row over Merril's dog had made them touchy to start with. Maybe, on account of that, he could excuse their manners; but he couldn't let things get unraveled right in the beginning either. It was best to nip it in the bud, before bad habits set in. They might think it a lark, but he didn't.

Still, it wasn't going so bad, he thought as they topped a rise and went down through a swale and past a greasewood bush where a butcher-bird had a mouse stuck on a twig. They were nearly to the northern end of the Valley now, and in another day they'd reach the Gila, and ease west some. Even that first day they'd made around ten miles, not bad when you considered the turmoil of the dog, and getting reorganized afterward.

No, it wasn't going too bad.

Anyhow, they'd got the Valley pretty near behind them now. Even after three days trailing, he found it hard to believe what the dry had done. Not that it was worse here than in the south—they were pretty much the same—but the bigness of it got you, the endless sweep of it, day in and out, unchanging as they passed through.

No matter where you looked the grass was gnawed or burned down to nothing. Cottonwood stands all had that papery dry look of death in their tops. Here and there arroyos cut down so sharply from the benches that nothing would fill them again— saving topsoil borne down on the run-off from the hills above. Here and there, too, the river had cut its banks down so far through its bed that growth along the edges had long since died off. Even the mesquite that crowded in to take the place of eaten and scorched grass had gone gray and black and brittle. It had deep, water-seeking roots, too. Then all about you saw the curving arch of glaring white ribs on the ground, the bones of cattle with now and then a scarecrow tatter of hide still clinging, with the innards having that dark, grainy look of old sawdust as the earth received them.

Seeing it all together day after day made him see taking off to hunt gold as a wiser thought than he knew. And it might be still wiser, whether gold was found or not, not to come back in the fall. Other parts of the country would be better; or no worse, anyhow.

Moreover, something told him that a few of the brands worn by that final gather of beef he'd peddled at the commissary at Huachuca had been smeared past prudence. What told him, you could call a sixth sense, and he didn't question it. Might be he'd got out in the nick of time.

Toward noon they reached a mudhole. They chivied off, the cows drawn there, their muzzles streaming brown ropes of wet; and after standing down to water out and eat, they lay beneath a straggle of *palo verde* for an hour. Later, going on, they climbed a steep, raggedy rise and, topping it, could make out at a far reach of the eye the raw scar of the Gila coming in its broad curves down to desert country from the Pinal Mountains lying northeast in the heat haze. Behind Harper, on sighting it, the others loosed a yell like men freed of prison, and he saw their caked and cracked lips spread in grins, with their teeth almost too white against the hide of sweat and dust that all wore.

They stood there for a space on top of the rise, letting the animals blow; then they began the long, easy slope leading downward to the plain, and Julius went to the tail of the line. Ahead of him for this stretch rode young Ross, then McGuire and Campbell, and at the head, the Merril kid. Back and forth along the line, the dog ran.

For a moment the sight of the fool dog chasing in such heat made him laugh in his mind. But in the next his mind drew up, frowning.

They oughtn't to have it, he thought, watching it run a gecko into a rock pile and there lose it, for all that it seemed to forage all right for itself without needing food from their supplies—as McGuire had been sure of, and Campbell, too. Even Ross had

had a head-shaking word over that, though more as an echo. Nor did it spook the animals any more, now that they were used to it.

Still, it was a bad thing. Maybe having it made Merril feel better—he'd been moping back there—but it had straight off caused a wrangle, and danged near bloodshed. Smoothed over now, you couldn't be sure it was really ended; the sight of the dog alone would be remindful.

It was queer how fast things developed sometimes, he thought, his mind going back three days and seeing in the strange early light what might have been a dog, and again a coyote, or loafer wolf, running them down. Maybe they should have known right off that no normal wild thing would do so; but how to tell it *was* normal? How to know it didn't have hydrophobia? Even a deermouse would run you down then. Dozing along, hearing Merril's shout and seeing that loping shape, why, you jumped at it.

He had anyhow. And McGuire had, too, and then McGuire had gone a jump beyond, and quicker than you knew was dragging out his carbine to shoot the thing down.

"It's Shep!" young Merril had yelled. "It's Shep!"

But McGuire, who didn't seem to hear, kept pulling at his carbine.

Merril yelled again, "It's Shep! Don't kill him, Pat!"

Pat paid no heed, however. Committed now, and going through the motions, he was deaf to Merril; and Merril finally saw that for himself, and with a last yell, "Goddam it, don't shoot!" he put his horse in a lunge at McGuire.

Even remembered calmly, Julius wasn't sure what happened next. Mostly it was all a boil of dust and yelling and gunfire and horses stampeding and bucking. All that stood clear was the gun slamming up when Merril hit it, Pat spilling from his horse, and the flame and roar in the quiet morning. But even that was run together with the horses rearing, the dog barking as in fun, and the dust lifting.

Finally, then, it slowed down; Pat lay on his back in the trail, and Merril was feeling him over for hurts.

"Goddam it, kid, you're lucky to be alive!" McGuire was shouting at him. "You're lucky your fool head wasn't blown off."

"I didn't aim to hurt you none," Merril said, pulling and hauling at him now. "It ain't as if I didn't say not to shoot, though."

"Goddam it!" Pat yelled. "How was I to know it was your dog? I took it for a hydraphoby wolf!"

"My God," Merril said, "I kept telling you! Can't you hear?"

"I don't hear the babble of every damned fool in the world!"

Ahead of Merril's answer, then, the dog itself came wagging over and made a pass at Pat's face with his tongue. Straight away Pat blew up all over again, lashing out with his boot and yelling, "Dog or no, I'd like to kill the damned thing, anyhow!" Hearing this, Merril then yelled, "Over my dead body!" and he let Pat go, so that he floundered back in the dust again.

Coming to this pass, the rest moved in to break it up. By littles, Pat let himself be hoisted up and turned about and dusted off. It then occurred to Julius that a pot of coffee might be good medicine, so he brewed a pot while the others brought in the drifted stock, and gathered up the scattered gear.

All told, this took near an hour that might better have been spent along the trail, but anyhow the trouble was finally smoothed over. Looking more like two ewes than humans, Pat and Ashley shook hands and even joked and laughed some over it. From all Julius could tell, the weather looked fair when they'd got started again.

Still, it was a misfortunate thing. Not only for the wrath of feeling stirred up, but for the lingering shadow that, as the saying went, readied the ground for small matters to grow up hairy and wild.

It gave a color to things in general, so that you grew watchful, and it made you look beneath something said for other meanings.

Take the little difference of opinion when they'd crossed the Tucson road. In planning the route Julius had meant the crossing of that road to be as natural as breathing. But no sooner did they stand astride it than Campbell asked him why they didn't take it.

"Why, shoot, there ain't no reason to," Julius said.

"It's better'n what we're on," Campbell said. "And once around the Rincons, it bends north, too."

"True enough on both counts," Julius said. "But it's longer, too. Don't forget we got to save time. Tucson'd cost a couple of days."

"What's two days in a month?" Campbell asked, eying him some. "Less risk of running out of water that way; be chances to buy feed, too, should we need it. We might even gain some time."

"You're just scared we'll all get drunk in town," Troy Ross said.

"Well, now you found me out," Julius said. "That's the nub of it."

It wasn't the nub, however. Mostly he was scared of being tailed from town, have these with him find out and quit. He knew highgraders from past experience, and they were rough people; as likely to work you over to learn where you headed as they were to wait until you'd found something.

But as the mention of that chance might scare them out of going, even on this trail, he'd been careful to keep it hidden.

Well, they took it good enough, grinned over it and forgot it—except maybe Campbell. Campbell seemed to watch him in an estimating manner, as if weighing things, and reaching some answer of his own. It made Julius wonder.

Which only went to show how a quarrel on one thing could make you edgy on others, no matter how different and innocent.

Except for the dog, the trail might never have raised a question.

Of course, the dog came in for its share of talk, too. Last night in camp, Pat brought that up, as you might know, from damaged pride, if no other reason; though he made it appear, sounding wise and solemn, that he had good reason.

"Seems to me it's going to be in the way," he said, while his coffee steamed and the campfire flickered.

"How do you figure that out?" young Merril asked.

"I guess it's shown us already," Pat said.

"It wasn't Shep that fired a gun and turned things upside down."

"It was on his account," Pat said. "But that ain't the point, anyhow. He's just in the way"—and here he moved his free hand in the air, showing how. "You ought to take him back."

"He wouldn't stay, if I did. He'd only follow again."

"Another mouth to feed," Campbell put in, as if his burden of hunting was already heavy when, as a fact, he hadn't yet shot anything. Of course, the country here was wrong for good game; but not too poorly for the rock squirrel killed and eaten by the dog an hour earlier.

That Merril should point this out didn't augur to improve the temper of the conversation none, though.

"Oh, it's rock squirrel, you want," Campbell said. "I can get all you want of that. I thought you wanted to eat human-style."

"I only meant that Shep could take care of himself," Merril said.

"I guess he could make trouble did we happen on Indians," Pat said, finding a new objection.

"Warn 'em we're about, you mean?" Merril said—then went on to answer himself. "He'd as easily warn *us*. Anyhow, such Indians as required our dog to tell of us ain't much to be scared of."

There was sense in that, Julius thought; more, at least, than on the other side of the same coin. But he knew that sense had nothing to do with it—not from McGuire's and Campbell's view, anyway.

"All the same," Pat said, glancing at Campbell for backing, "be a lot better was you to take him home."

"Aye to that," Campbell said. "Going light, you could easy catch us in a few days." Then, as if to get a vote, he said, "How 'bout you, Troy?"

"Well ..." Troy began, but then he didn't say after all, but of a sudden made it appear that the fire needed poking, that the coffee needed heating, and his seat needed shifting. It was funny how he likened himself to those two, yet hung fire in something like this.

It was Merril who took Troy off the hook, though maybe too involved in it to see that Troy was on a hook.

"If I go back with him," he said quietly, "I stay there."

Well, it was easy to see that no one had looked for that. They were simply in a nit-picking mood that had gone runaway. Except that it was poor doings for the dog to be the middle of a wrangle, Julius had no feeling for it. Maybe it was best gone, but not on those terms.

So he said, hoping it would prove out, "I'll take the damned hound home. Seeing I'm nothing to him, he might not follow me back. Of course"—and here he slid his glance about—"it would take me longer than a younger man, maybe five or six days, going good."

Well, it worked, for they wouldn't hear of that. McGuire and Campbell and Ross hooted and slapped their legs and bawled out, "No, by God! To hell with that!"—glad for an easy way out of a bad thing, and McGuire and Campbell maybe pleased to know he *might* have gone, if they'd agreed. Only Ash didn't join in, and sat poking a stick at the fire and scowling. But he'd come out of it with his mutt still with him, and would cheer up in time.

All things considered, they weren't too bad, Julius thought as they made their way along the ridges and hogbacks that eased them down to the Gila, still away in tomorrow. Young and full of beans, they were quick to stand up to each other, but he guessed they'd work out.

True, there was in his mind a few little things that stood no bigger than shadows just now and would bear watching; but he'd face whatever might come of them when the time arrived.

The main thing was the hunting of gold. So long as nothing blocked that, they could carry on as they pleased. But if the hunt was put in danger of any kind, there was nothing he wouldn't do to prevent it.

In past times he'd seen men killed for that reason. And as this was his party and plan, and maybe his last chance for a strike, he was ready and willing to do so himself.

CHAPTER FIVE

They'd left their horses below in a draw, and climbed now on foot with Campbell leading along a trail no wider than a hair. On McGuire's left, the naked flank of the mountainside threw at him a heat as stunning and raw as what came out of an ore roaster; while on his right, the trail fell off so sudden and far down that only a glance chilled him. And whenever he made himself look out and away at the thin crawling line that made its slow way across the white desert plain toward the strung-out straggle of dark that would be salt cedars and such along the banks of the Rio Salado, why, his legs almost buckled.

The feeling gave him a sense of smallness and weakness before the world; and the knowing, and how it worked upon the aloneness that seemed always with him, angered him. It didn't help any that Campbell didn't appear to notice either the drop or the blast of heat, though his shirt was almost black with sweat. Simply to see how Campbell plowed on, looking neither one side or the other, but always at the trail for sign, was enough to make him call, "How d'you know this here's a sheep trail?"

He'd asked the same thing three times in half an hour, and this time Campbell didn't bother to turn about.

" 'Cause Julius said it was," he called over his shoulder. "Anyhow, I seen the tracks about a minute back. Didn't look like nothing else."

Pat hadn't seen any himself, but he didn't let on to Jack. "So, what if we did? They could easy be a week old."

"Didn't look so to me," Campbell answered. "You don't figure to look for sheep where sign ain't, do you?"

There was no way to answer that without looking foolish, and Pat didn't. Jack was always making fun of him, anyhow, though he didn't mind it too much so long as no one else heard. Being that Jack let him go about with him mostly made up for it.

Today, however, high on this crazy mountain, trying to find wild sheep in a hammer of desert heat way worse than anything on the San Pedro, such talk only made him feel smaller and more alone than ordinary.

"Tracks or no," he called out, "I'd rather old Diamond-Hitch himself go chase sheep."

That time there was no reply. Putting that tag on Julius had got a laugh from Jack before, but there was none now, just silence, as if he hadn't heard. Likely he was already thinking of something different from sheep. He was like that, Jack was, his mind always running ahead and beyond and around. Pat would think a thought right into the earth and then bury it; but not Jack. Jack was like a good fist-fighter with his thoughts, always moving, seeing things behind things.

Or maybe, Pat began to think, he *had* heard, but didn't see it as a joke any more. That was like him, too; he always liked his own jokes best. For a moment the knowing of that little weakness of Jack's made him grin, but then the feeling of the day began to bear down again.

All right, he thought, let Jack keep to himself. He could do the same; and for a space of a dozen yards he walked along with his shoulders unbent to the climb, his eyes intent upon the trail and his carbine at the ready, his mind closed down to all else, showing how he, too, could be withdrawn and stride on steady and strong and uncaring.

Then, as he was looking so hard at the trail, he failed to see when Jack reached a fork and drew to a halt. By the time he found out, he'd walked straight into his back with a jar so hard that his carbine fell to the ground in a clatter of metal and stone. "Goddam it to hell!" he shouted.

Campbell caught his balance and turned about.

"For Christ's sake, can't you see?"

Pat bent over, reaching down for his carbine. A week ago the Merril kid had asked was he deaf. Now Jack asked if he was blind. "It's this goddam scrawl of a trail we're on," he said. "It ain't fit for bugs to travel."

But Campbell didn't care how it happened. In that same steamy tone, he said, "There'll be no sheep on the mountain if you don't control yourself."

McGuire tried again to explain that it was being intent upon those sheep himself that had caused the collision. But Jack wasn't listening. He was looking at the fork, and at the sign following both prongs.

"You don't like the trail we're on, take your choice here," he said. "There's tracks on both prongs; not much difference in either."

Pat made an effort and looked, and for the first time really saw tracks, pointed and splayed out and, except that they were some wider, like an antelope's. One prong went straight, almost level with the fork, while the second went screeching upward in a pitch that seemed twice as steep as that already climbed. From what he could tell, it went right on up and over the ridgepole of the mountain.

He'd be damned to hell if he'd go that way; but when he glanced at Jack, he knew it wasn't his choice, after all. Jack's smile was sly, holding a dare, and the hint of a bet that Pat wouldn't take it.

It being one of those days when he almost hated Jack, he knew he'd have to take that trail, even if it half killed him. Past doubt, Jack would otherwise laugh him all the way back to camp.

He motioned to the left. "It'll do," he said and, holding his carbine, he turned and stepped out before Jack could say something smart.

If he thought the climb had been steep before, it was only because he'd never before faced one like this—not even as a mucker in the mines of Silver City or Tombstone or Bisbee.

It was even worse than it looked from the fork, shooting up in straight lines against the face of the mountain. It was needful that he use his hands, too, now, as well as his feet, to dig and gouge at the rock, and to pull himself along by grabbing hold of such brush that might bear his weight. Even to rest he had to wedge himself in to keep from slipping back down.

According to Julius, this heave of rock was called the Sierra Estrella, after the Spanish, and meant the Mountain of the Star; but Pat was willing to bet that no Spaniard had ever set foot on it, name or no. Likely they'd just stood below and looked up, having had more sense than to take the beating that he was. And tracks or no tracks, he was nearly ready to bet that no mountain sheep would climb this thing, either—for all their feet had little suction cups to prevent slipping. At least, that's what Julius said, if it wasn't another of his tales.

Maybe fifteen minutes had passed when he heaved himself above a saguaro, and there sat down and braced himself while he took a pull from his canteen. Looking back down, he saw the thin trail weaving and plunging beneath until it reached the fork where it grew more level. The fork was way down, farther than he'd thought, and when his eye went out the second prong and in time found Jack, why, he looked no bigger than an ant. Even from so far, he could see Jack's long legs pumping him along with no effort at all; and the sight, when thought of against his own torture, made him mad all over again.

Just at that moment Jack turned and without breaking stride waved in his direction. He couldn't have known where Pat was, but the mere suspicion that he might have known was scary; and the way that he waved, easy and no doubt laughing, made Pat still madder.

Well, to hell with you, too, Jack, he thought as he pulled himself up and climbed ahead. You and your smile and sly tricks. Yes, and calling me names and making fun of me. Goddam, you even laughed when Merril's horse knocked me overboard last week. I heard.

"You better be careful, Jack," he breathed out, while sweat leaked itching down on his cheeks. "There's things I know about you that others would like to know. Maybe you forgot the little lie I told for you in court in Mesilla; what saved you from a stretched neck, or a stretch of time in Santa Fe prison, anyhow. Maybe you figure that five years back is too far for folks to remember, and that an old man killed for seven dollars would be gone from memory anyhow. But I remember. And others would like to know what I remember."

He stumbled, and his breath ran out; but his thoughts went on.

You like folks to think you're just an ordinary hand, name of Jack Campbell. But I know different. Lest you forget, a fellow called Ed Post is looking over your shoulder.

For a second or two the vision of how that information would strike those he might give it to filled him with a pleasure so fierce that it stood above the sobering fact of the perjury charge that would surely follow, and the even more sobering fact of having to deal with Campbell himself. Or Post, for he would then be Post once more.

But he soon remembered, and the pleasure left him. In its place stood doubt that he could ever do a thing like that, not only for those fearful reasons, but for the added fear of losing Jack. The day of trial in the fly-blown, airless Mesilla courtroom had wound their lives together; and his sudden inspiration on the stand had bailed Jack out of trouble and kept them bound, like plaited rope, ever since.

Up to then, he'd hardly known Jack, saving by reputation and sight, and a careful howdy on the streets now and then. But it was Pat's way to look about him, and he'd learned enough to know that Jack had what he liked in a man; what he hadn't, himself, nor ever would.

Even in that hostile court, bound in irons and with armed men about, Jack had disregarded all that went on. Jack would never worry over what men saw in him, fret about his size and looks, or how to make out in the world.

Clawing up this scorching mountain, Pat remembered how the sight had pulled at him, worked upon him and set his mind turning. Maybe his thoughts had spun out while the testimony piled up, maybe he could never be the man that Jack was; but by putting Jack in his debt, he'd have a place in his shadow. Maybe it was blind fate that set him down where he could witness Jack's outrage. But it was the sudden knowing of how to guide and twist odd chance into a bigger and different kind of chance that had turned his tongue and brought a mistrial about.

As well he might be, Jack was surprised, and he hadn't understood at first, either. But little by little, as Pat hit him for loans, as Pat asked his help against the town bullies, and as Pat began to tail him through the countryside from one job to the next—in the mines, riding for a cow spread, or whatever they might find along the Rio Grande, and more lately southern Arizona—he understood. In time, he did.

All told, they'd got on pretty well together, too. Pat gave him no trouble and never riled him with open talk of his debt. Campbell came to see that Pat just wanted to run with him, and he learned to live with it.

Any way he cut it, McGuire's company beat the gallows.

Lately, however, there'd been a change. Campbell's jokes seemed honed finer; he poked fun at Pat more, too. Sometimes he blazed up in a boil of anger that seemed to deny what Pat held over him. He called him names. He was sly and open by turn, making Pat guess his thoughts. Often, too, he was silent and blank of eye for periods so long that Pat could only wonder where his mind traveled.

It seemed to have started with their landing at the Ross place, and having old Julius harangue them on goldhunting. It was as if the yarning, day in and out, set Jack's mind wandering off to new ideas and places. The one fear in Pat's mind these years had been that Jack might one day leave him; but with drought obliging them to eke along from day to day, and no money in hand, it hadn't been a big one. Jack would know that pulling out would call for plenty of money to cover his tracks right. Poverty had certain blessings for Pat.

But now this change had come. It was almost as if Jack had hold of such money, or scented it. For himself, Pat didn't believe they'd find gold—his luck had never run that way—but Jack, since crossing the Tucson road, at least, seemed to think they might. While Pat couldn't guess what might have passed between Jack and Julius then, Jack appeared to get a notion that this journey had more point to it than chance searching.

In view of Jack's ways lately that could mean only one thing. On filling his poke with gold, he'd cut and run. Up there in that wild northern wilderness, far from those who'd like to hear Pat's tale, it would be easy. At any time, he could just disappear without a trace.

The thought so filled him that he hardly knew he was topping out on the ridgepole of the mountain. He made the last few yards and, coming onto a clutter of rotten granite, stood surprised to be suddenly in the middle of so reaching an emptiness.

Then it scared him, and the aloneness in him was made bigger by the sight and feel of the aloneness all about. Up here on this rocky spine, no air moved. The heat came pounding at him from the sky and bare stone alike. The glitter from the desert, far, far down, but going out to all the world's edges, sawed at his eyes. Never had he felt his smallness so, never so cut off from living, from being alive. It was almost like being dead, but knowing it, too.

The crush of it made him weak and he moved to a rock and, with his canteen under him, let himself down. To the north and far out, the others were moving in to make camp among the trees by the river; laughing, no doubt, and joking, feeling frisky to have the day's grind over. Troy and Merril would be horsing around in the water, likely, and Julius would be yelling for them to help him fix camp, or maybe already yarning—about the Lost Adams Diggings, or the Lost Mexican Ledge—in order to keep the gold fever high. Well, maybe not.

Anyhow there'd be no thought for him up here on this blistering mountain. He could yell until he fell over, but they wouldn't hear him. He could burn up all his ammunition, and they wouldn't hear that either. He could die and draw down buzzards to feast, and they'd never know. They might behold the circle of planing wings that spiraled down, but after a shrug they'd continue their pleasure by the water.

Goddam them, anyhow, he thought. He'd like to shoot them all, every last one. It was plain impulse that brought his carbine up level, but reasoned intent held it there. It didn't matter that a bullet wouldn't reach them; there was something real in sighting on the far camp, while his mind picked over the order of killing.

It would be Merril first; him or his damned dog. Then old Julius, and then Troy. And then, while he was at it, he might arrange to take Jack, too. Somewhere along his backtrail, he could wait for him.

Just then, as the pleasure of having Jack in his sights was growing bigger, a sound touched his ear. It came from behind him, and could barely be heard for its stealing softness. It came and went like a bird, and might never have been at all, saving that he sensed a presence there, too.

The maker of that sound was still there. He could *feel* it there, watching him.

In a slow move, he began to turn; then midway around he stopped and his body filled with snowmelt. What had been no more than a crazy notion of killing Jack had turned about in his mind and enlarged to make it possible that Jack was stalking *him*.

It was Jack behind him, there. Jack was going to kill him on this mountain top, and be free of him.

It was too real a thought for him to put down. In a wild yell, he jumped to his feet and swerved and fired all in one motion— hearing the roar of the carbine and the wide *screee* of the bullet spanging off of stone into air. But it wasn't Campbell, at all, that in a flick of movement passed from sight beyond a high point of rock. It was only a sheep, old and rangy and gray, its coat in patches and one horn bent off sidewise. It was there and gone.

"Oh, my God!" he said; and his body began to shake, to shake with sudden relief, with the gladness of being wrong, and with knowing of his own foolishness.

Then he said, in half a sob, "Oh, Jesus!" and slumped down onto the rock, and put his face in his hands.

CHAPTER SIX

For Troy the days came and went, the sharp edge of dawn swelling into full light and on toward the blue, milky heat of noon and afternoon, the brassy plate of the sun creeping through its hours across the arching sky until it sank from sight in a bath of red and turquoise and gold, and dusk seeped up out of the earth like smoke and grew into night where stars as hard and cold as ice winked down on yellow fingers of campfires.

The land passed, too. The deserts were a week behind them now, the grainy plains and bare-hided mountains that all day soaked in the sun's scorching, and all night gave it off; where no shade occurred except at rivers and sometimes in draws and the dry beds of creeks; where life went on mostly at night, and that seen by day, quail and dove as a rule, appeared in the early and late hours.

The rivers went their way, flowing or not, but marking the miles in any case: the Arivaipa, the Gila, the Salt, the Agua Fria, one called by Julius the New River; creeks, too, nameless and dusty, some of them.

This was mesa country that they traveled through now, somewhat higher than the sun-white haze that drowned the desert plains and valleys far to the rear, and almost three weeks and something like two hundred miles and more from home. Mesas lined out against a robin's egg sky like stairsteps, their tops flat and sharp in the clear air. Closer they raised grama fetlock high on the animals, and put up stands of prickly pear, too, and bayonet.

There were mountains here, too, beyond the mesas, but seen so far off and softly that they might have only been thought of. Those on the right, anyhow, and to the rear and ahead. On the left they were closer, ten miles maybe, and rose from a canyon that lay between the mesa and the foothills of the mountains. Julius called them the Bradshaws, and their heights were marked with pine trees.

The days in their passing had a pattern that made it easy to lose one in the other, as they seemed to flow together, so that Thursday might turn out to be Monday, or Saturday, after thought—if anyone bothered to think. But all were alike, and no one different from the next except for the change in the country.

First light, or even while dark still held, they were out of their blankets. Wood gathered the previous evening was stacked and lit and, while Julius organized breakfast, the others would bring in the stock from picket or hobbles and start rigging the packs. With breakfast over, the gear settled firm, and Pat and Jack easing off in the dawn to hunt, the day's march would begin, work step by step toward noon, when they would stop to rest and eat, then go onward once more until afternoon bled into dusk, and they'd make camp again; and after eating and all such, would roll up in their blankets while the stars hardened above them and Julius went on about the Lost Tayopa or the Lost Frenchman, his voice growing fainter and fainter until it joined the night.

Troy liked it. He liked the freedom, the don't-care and the don't-have-to-care. He liked to look at the country without feeling indebted to it for his livelihood, or responsible for or questioning what happened in it. It was good just to pass through and not bother his head about how many cows it might feed, and for how long; whether or not it would rain, and when, and all else that living at home had made him do. Sometimes, on thinking back, it seemed his whole life had passed in worry over such things, in barely scraping by, and in watching Matt and his ma and Lilly worry and barely scrape by.

Out here with the wilderness grown deeper each day, he needn't bother with such. He felt well rid of them, and aimed to keep it that way. There even entered his mind now and again—and more often as the miles from home mounted—the notion of not returning at all.

Times when Ashley wasn't about were easiest for such ideas. Ash, however, and especially since reaching this higher, grassy land, always had some way of relating it with what they'd left behind. Near all they saw here, or that happened, made him look back.

A particularly tasty-looking stand of grama would set him off. "Look at that side-oats, Troy," he'd say; or blue, or black, or whatever kind of grama it was. "That'd sure weight up a herd in a hurry. I'd bet the sight of that would make Matt's eyes bug out."

Troy didn't have to look to know how fast a herd would gain; nor did he doubt that Matt's eyes would bug out. But he didn't want to think about the grass in that way.

Or maybe it was an afternoon thunderstorm in the Bradshaws. "Hey, Troy!" Ash would say, not able to let that be either. "Look at that rain pouring down! Like a curtain! By God, Pa should see!" Then he might pause, and add, "No, maybe not; he'd only feel bad."

But Troy didn't want to think about the rain in that way either. Doing so was only one step from remembering Matt on the gallery looking at the rainless mountains of home. He disliked reminders of home.

Sometimes just a thought wandering loose in Ashley's head would set him off. It needn't be daylight either. They could be lying in their blankets, waiting for sleep.

Then he might say, "I wonder why there's rain and grass here, and not back home?"

It never paid to ignore him, as he'd only repeat it.

"My God, Ash," Troy would finally say, "I don't know. Let's get some sleep."

But that only fueled the fire, and Troy would hardly get settled again before Ash'd say, "I'll bet that's part of it—the distance."

No more than ignoring him did it help to pretend sleep either. Someone else—Julius, say—would answer, and it'd just spread out more.

"You want to remember there's a heap of mountains between here and there," he'd say in the dark. "We're higher here, too; the country in general is higher. Height draws the wet."

"You figure that's it?"

"Partly. And as to grass, don't forget that this ain't ever seen a cow, while that down there's seen nothing but. Pulling all the stock from that valley down there for a time would make a difference."

"Be no point in living there then," Ash would say.

"Not much less than now," Julius'd point out. "Besides, once the grass comes back, the range could be restocked. Maybe some kind of special blood, a breeding animal, say."

"It would still need rain," Ash would say, going back to that again, as if Julius's notions were too strange and novel to deal with.

"Well, you'd need some, sure. But a lot'd depend on whether the grass was let to grow awhile, or gobbled up straight off."

They'd go on in this manner for fifteen or twenty minutes across Troy's body with what began as one of Ashley's simple-minded thoughts; until Troy would bury his head in his arms to keep it out of his ears.

But still hearing, and worse—having what he didn't want to think of go on spinning and turning in his head long after all talk had ended.

All told he guessed it was wrong that Ashley had been asked along, and if it hadn't been for Campbell, Troy could have told him he wasn't wanted. But even at that early date, when serious talk was just beginning, Jack had known that Ash was needed for the food he could bring. Not that Troy found fault with Jack's thinking ahead; he admired it.

But even so, he wished they hadn't asked Ash, for all it would have meant more begging of supplies from Matt and from Ma; and even snitching some when they weren't looking, as he'd been obliged to do.

Still, it would've been worth it, just to be rid of him. He was such a kid; a nuisance at best, and at worst downright dangerous.

If it wasn't his talk of the country and all, he was noticing that Troy often took the manners of Campbell and McGuire — mimicking and sneering. He'd bawled in the dark on leaving— Troy'd seen—and an hour later had come close to blows or worse with Pat. There was his dog, too, that had brought *that* on; and just as bad in some way was its knack for finding food, no matter how poor Jack and Pat found the hunting.

You could easy tell they didn't like that; no man would.

Just now, today, and for the last few days, there was Ash's burro to give them trouble. Owing to the desert heat, a hoof had split, and now it was lame in one leg, the pastern oozing; all of which caused Ash to lag behind, catching up only at noon and evening. Mostly it was only half a mile or so, but although Ash said he didn't mind and wasn't scared, it bothered Troy. He knew the others didn't like it either, and as with all else that Ash did, or didn't do, he felt it weigh on *him*.

For the fourth time in an hour, he turned about in his saddle and looked behind him across the land.

When he came front again, Julius glanced at him. "You see him back there yet?"

"Not yet. Seen him last about thirty minutes ago."

Julius poked his beard at a juniper tree ahead that somehow had managed to grow all alone in country it didn't really belong in. "We might pull up there in the shade a space until he shows."

It seemed important to Troy that he be unconcerned about Ash, or that he seem unconcerned. But three days of it was enough.

"I don't doubt he'll be along," he said. "No point in slowing, just because we can't see him every minute." He looked westerly, at the Bradshaws, now tailing out in their northern foothills. "Pat and Jack are over there somewhere; could be near abreast of him."

Julius didn't answer that remark, but rode on looking ahead toward a valley that breasted broad and white a great way off. Julius called it Lonesome Valley, and the range that rose beyond it still too far and blue to make out well, the Black Hills. Only this morning, as the mesas bled off into the shoulders of the Bradshaws, had they begun to see them; no doubt, they'd cross them in a few days.

After a time Julius said, "I been thinking Ashley might better shoot that burro."

"I mentioned it more'n once," Troy said, though this wasn't exactly true. But he'd nodded when Campbell and McGuire brought it up.

"For all we keep ahead of him, it still slows us down," Julius said. "Moreover, lagging, he could have real trouble some time."

"Might teach him a lesson to have some," Troy said.

"Maybe. Trouble's often fatal though. Be best to shoot it before trouble comes."

They came to the tree and drew up. Close to five minutes went by, but Ashley didn't appear.

Finally Julius poked his beard at the peak of the Bradshaws, where dark cloud lay, as on most afternoons. It was far back now, but you could still see the rain, shifting and gray, and sometimes hear thunder.

"Run-off should be coming down now," he said. "Back some we crossed a wash that's going to get it. If Ash ain't over it yet he'll likely need help." Julius stood down and arranged himself on his butt beneath the tree. "Wouldn't hurt for you to look while I rest my bones."

"All right," Troy said, for all he'd like to rest his own bones. But he didn't care to argue with Julius. Under his tales and easy way, a certain toughness showed now and then that never had shown at home.

"All right," he said again, and necked his horse about, though after going some yards he wished he *had* argued some if only for show. No doubt he'd agreed too quick; and the knowing of that, along with the reason for going at all, made him more put out than ever with Ashley.

"Goddam him!" he said. "Holding us up and making us wonder!" Admitting this wonder aloud, and admitting inside a small thread of worry, didn't help either.

The wash would be around twenty minutes back, he thought. They'd come along at a walk, however—and he loped on the backtrail. Riding with his eyes on the Bradshaws, while he wondered if the wash was filled yet, soon turned his mind toward home and Matt, and what he'd think to see such rain. The question stayed in his mind until he came in sight of the fringe of pear and brush that marked the wash—and that, too, was Ashley's doing. But for him, Troy would never have thought of Matt or home at this time.

"It'd serve him right if he *is* caught! I hope he is!"

He rode with that in his mind until, at a point no more than a hundred and fifty yards from the brush, he happened to glance at the foothills again, and caught sight of Campbell and McGuire coming out of them. They were distant yet, and there was still no sign of Ash, but he stopped to wait anyway.

They caught his wave, and in five minutes drew up. It being a day when they rode light of game, they looked glum. But they cheered up when he told them his errand.

"You can't tell," Jack said, "he might be caught. Rain chased us out of the hills."

"We could trail along to see the fun," Pat said, "if there is any."

Riding on, they soon reached the wash and looked below. It was wide and flat, and went down from the banks some four or five feet, though they were broken down where the string had gone through earlier. It was almost twenty yards across, and sure enough, Ashley and the burro were out in the middle, the burro down and Ash working to tail it up. The calico stood off unconcerned, and the dog sat nearby, watching the doings.

Under the far bank a trickle of water had already started to run, coming down from the hills.

Troy watched it stream along behind Ash, and even swell some, and called out, "You're going to get wet, if you don't start moving, kid."

Ash stopped cranking on the tail and looked up. "I aim to get this burro up first. I don't mind a little wet anyhow."

"You could be caught in a real gully-washer," Troy called.

"I'll hear it in time," Ash said. "We were making out fine until it broke down here. Only need to get it walking again."

"I've yet to see that burro pick a decent quitting place," Jack said.

Not answering, Ash set again to cranking on the tail. Nothing happened, though, beyond the burro hee-hawing and the water streaming wider.

"You should have shot it long since," McGuire called.

"I ain't so quick to get a gun out," Ash said.

"Be saving a heap of trouble, if you was," Pat fired back.

"Beyond talk, I note the trouble ain't concerned you any."

Pat's whiskery flews filled out with wind, but while he was getting his words in order, the horses raised their ears and turned their heads west. From afar there came a deep sound like a waterfall. Troy noticed that the water had spread out almost to the burro's tail.

He felt fidgety, and shouted, "Ash, you better get out of there while you can! You ain't got much time!"

While not answering, it was plain that Ash heard, and that he heard the sound, too. He gave the tail a few more wild jerks and then, seeing the water now streaming at his heels, dropped the tail and began to fiddle with the kyack bindings.

Up on the bank, where he could see the water grow and hear the thunder of the main body clearly now, Troy felt in half a fright. The fastenings were on the burro's downside, and Ash was taking forever.

He turned to Campbell. "You reckon we ought to help?" he said, hoping that Jack would say yes.

But he didn't. He shook his head and chewed on a stem of grass. "He'll make it. Learn a lesson on holding us up, too."

As Troy had talked along this line to Julius, it went against his grain to change his mind. So he went around it, asking about the burro.

"To hell with it," Pat put in. "Saved, it's no good anyhow."

"Besides," Jack pointed out, "he ain't asked for no help."

That was true, Troy thought, even though he knew that Ash was too bull-headed to ask, after all the ribbing and haggling.

But he needed it now. The kyack wouldn't free. One strap was clear but the other was too far under to reach. On his knees, Ash dug and scrabbled around in the water that now ran bank to bank. Troy was almost on the point of going down, however weak he might look to Pat and Jack, when Jack yelled, "There she comes!"

Troy turned and looked, and it was true. The wash ran straight for two hundred yards, and up at the turn the water came—water and mud and foam, brush, parts of trees and rock, all roaring on together in a moving wall that leaped and tossed in the sunlight.

Troy stood as if he had been struck a blow. Then he turned and yelled at Ash—any help except warning him was too late now—"Ash! Ash!"—while he pointed, and the roar hammered.

But the sound had warned Ash, too. Shooting a glance that way, he came to his feet. From the kyack, he jerked his war-bag and flour sack and slung them, their necks tied, around his own. He shooed the dog to the bank and ran for his calico horse, which still waited.

For Troy, now, it all slowed down. Rather than make for the bank, too, Ash shook a loop into his rope and, turning past the burro, leaned and slid it onto the forelegs, then straightened and drove forward. Behind the burro went into a panic of bawling and thrashing as it was dragged along.

Ash almost made it all the way, but not quite. The horse charged up, eyes rolling, ears flat; its hoofs slashed in the shaking earth of the bank and bore it onward into the brush. Then what seemed to Troy to have slowed, stopped entirely. The horse had just topped out when, all at once, the torrent and pound of water smashed behind it. Into his sight came the burro, borne aloft; the rope, taut as a drawn bowstring; the calico, jerking to his hind legs on the brink and teetering; and then, seen as lightning, Ash's belt knife in a flicker that cut the line at the bow of the saddle.

Then it moved again—the flood slammed on, the horse came onto its forefeet and moved ahead from the peeling bank. Troy felt his innards turn watery with relief; then, on sighting Ash's face, he was reminded that the burro had been swept away, and that he might have helped.

Being Ash's doing that laid him open so, his head went into a boil, and ahead of thought, he stepped out toward him and shouted up, "You didn't ask for help! You didn't ask, goddam it!"

From his drawn face, Ashley turned a white glance on them all, then it settled on Troy. "I didn't think I had to—not of you!"

He then rode off ahead, alone, while Troy stood watching, feeling empty, yet full, too, of a misery of hate. It was easy for him to think that, with those sacks slung over his front, Ashley could easily pass for some drippy-bottomed, melon-busted woman.

CHAPTER SEVEN

To Campbell's ear, the woods held no sound; it had been quiet as death since Pat had shot his doe fifteen or twenty minutes ago when the crash of the gun had silenced everything. He could even hear his heart, though it seemed to work harder up here than in lower country, anyway. Here in what were called the Black Hills, they were past a mile up, higher than any time since leaving home; or what he called home—though he'd had none since kid days ten years ago.

He was sitting a few yards off a game trail, backed against a ragged stand of manzanita, with only his eyes moving. Some folks, when hunting, thought it smart to hide behind things; but as they had to move to look, they often scared game. Or else they went noising through the woods like a herd drive—Pat's way, unless cautioned.

But not him. He liked to sit in front of cover where he could see without bobbing up and down. That way the deer almost never saw you until too late; it was motion that drew their eye.

Sitting to face west, with the early slanting sun behind him, he could see all that mattered. On his right, uphill, the deer run passed through piñon and juniper, holding in sight for nearly a hundred yards until it went into jackpine. Beyond a deep belt of this, he made out the reaching, stilly tops of bigger pine, as big around as a man, that took over and crowned the mountain top.

Off on his left, downgrade, the cover changed. For some way below, knots of oak and juniper and piñon grew, but soon the chapparal took over, and in time the slope ran solid in mountain laurel and manzanita.

On his left, too, and by stretching his neck, he could see out over the brush and foothills into the far ocean of grass that was Lonesome Valley. See into yesterday, he thought; and even the day before that—crossing had taken them two days.

Also left, but no more than a hundred yards, was where Pat had finally managed to bag a deer. Recalling how Pat had jumped up, yelling, "I got it! I got it!" he was just as glad that Pat had killed first and gone back to join the others ahead of him. He'd rather hunt alone than with others, anyway, especially with Pat—a man too noisy for the woods. He'd gone strangely owly, too, lately, and would be poor company while waiting for the forest to get over its scare.

From afar now there came the metal *cheekity-cheekity* of a squirrel. Another answered, sounding like swearing; then a blue jay called.

Sitting as still as he could, he made his eyes move still more carefully over the game trail. Now would be the time; almost any minute, one would come stepping by. He felt excited and almost a boy again, hunting deer back in the far-off Palo Duro Canyon with his old man. That was back a way! Only in time, though, and place. The feeling was similar—the sense of wilderness reaching about, the tingling stretch of the waiting and the knowing that, just now, there was nothing else he'd rather be doing.

Just then, as he came to that thought, a deer showed. For the smallest part of a second, he might have been in the Palo Duro; but in the next part he was back in the Black Hills of Arizona, and the deer was nearing like a shadow from the jack-pines above.

He sat still more quietly than before, and watched it float along the grade, breathing shallow, and slitting his eyes; deer knew when they were stared at and grew nervous. Since it could see his gun lift as the moment came, he wanted to have it close.

It eased along unsuspecting, browsing on leaves and twigs in the trail. In the velvet now, the antlers at seventy yards were blurred, but soon he saw it was a buck of eight points, not counting brow tines. The coat was in the red, natural for summer, though some black showed beneath. As in a muley, the ears fanned out as big as shovels.

Now! a part of him said; but another part said, no—and he held himself in. No need to rush, as the deer, at thirty yards now, was still coming; he could see the polished hoofs and hear the jaws working.

At twenty yards it stopped while its ears and wet nose tested sound and odor; antsy now, but still unknowing of him, though its eyes passed over him twice. Each time they did so, he stopped everything he could control until the glance moved on.

Then, when it started browsing again, there was no more waiting. Almost without thought, he raised the gun and fired at the shoulder point. The buck had seen the move, as he'd guessed it might, and as it leaped and turned and lit running, he levered up another round against need. But at fifty yards upgrade, the forelegs broke down, and five yards farther on the deer sprawled over and lay still.

In the patch of sunlight that fell upon it there, the coat looked golden as it shimmered above relaxing muscle and nerve.

He bled and cleaned the deer and, after spreading the rib cage with a stick for cooling, brought his horse in from a copse a quarter mile off. Then, loading and going ahead with the reins, he set off on a line that would bring him to the other men in an hour or so.

All about him again silence closed down, the only sounds made by himself and the horse upon the soft earth. He was going slightly upgrade and northeast, according to the sun, which now came quartering over the low tops of piñon and juniper. He felt it on his face and all along his right side in a soft warmth that was pleasant after sitting in cool shade so long. He felt a trickle of sweat beginning on his flanks, too.

It was good to feel the sweat and the sun and to be out in the early quiet, alone save for the horse, and with the deer whose hunting and end had been thought out well, not just stumbled onto and shot in a flurry. He had his good days and bad ones, and he guessed that today, so far at least, was better than most he'd had in some time. Maybe since leaving the Palo Duro country.

Well, maybe it was, and for a moment his mind turned on those times, seeing in them all that a knowing man would want, and seeing too the fool, headstrong boy who'd thrown them over in favor of seeking what he took for bigger things elsewhere; things that only brought him grief and trouble, and in the long run settled out in a brawl that left him with a clouded freedom and an alias.

Well, that was hindsight for you. But no kid could know ahead where stubbornness might lead, for all he'd had advice— maybe too much for his nature. And time he'd learned it was too late to undo wrong, to go back, to start over again where he'd left off. Seeing it in its true light, a man was apt to turn his back on thoughts of change, and drift along with the current, the easy way.

Today seemed different though, he thought, as he crossed a patch of grass and let the horse graze slowly over it. The Palo Duro was long gone in the past, his people dead and the old place sold for taxes. But there could still be something for him somewhere.

Likely it was the day that made the thought so strong. That was natural. His mood was open to it, and the country here made such ideas easier than down south where all was drought and bad times. No man hankered to start on his own in those conditions; nor could easy think of fairer land, either, it wore on him so. One like himself, anyhow.

But he guessed the bud had opened with Julius's gold talk. Then maybe it had grown bigger and more hopeful when their crossing the Tucson road had made it seem certain that Julius led them to a strike; maybe even to a sure thing found long before, that only needed the right time and men to work it. Why else should he bypass towns?

Now up here in the smiling Black Hills, far from all troublesome times and places, alone with his deer and good feeling, it seemed possible enough. And after an hour of dwelling on it in detail, the sight of grass and cattle and water that his share of the lode would buy came to be close at hand, and even real again, as in childhood days.

At just about that time, he came to a hump of broken rock, and rounding it, looked into a sandy draw at what seemed to be horse tracks. Below, he found that they were; and, pushing along faster than before, came up in fifteen or twenty minutes with the others where they lay resting in a glade of the big pines.

"Give me an hour, and there's a chance I'll show you something interesting," Julius said as they headed into the timber again.

There were some catcalls in answer to this, which Julius ignored; then McGuire turned to Campbell. "Likely some tree that he watered out against one time."

Campbell looked at Pat, and smiled in good humor. In his good-day mood, Pat's crude jokes didn't bother him; he even felt kindly toward him. If ever he found a place of some kind, he might even take Pat on. "I can't think what else it might be," he said.

For a second Pat's eye held that small worry that asked if Campbell poked fun at him; then the pointed, whiskery face grinned. "Unless it's a pile of dung he unloaded once," Pat said.

"Well, that's another thought," Campbell said. "Bigger, too."

This made Pat laugh outright, his mouth a hole in his mat of a beard, where yellow and brown teeth showed, half rotten. Then, as if it was too much that Jack be so agreeable, the eye came searching again.

"You're sure in a gay mood," he said.

"Why not?" Campbell said. "It's a fine-looking morning, and I got a fine-looking buck to match."

"Some better'n a doe, I guess," Pat said, as if he had to go on seeking fault, even if it wasn't in plain view.

"I ain't said that. A doe's got better meat any day."

As if hunting a trap, Pat thought that over a time; but before he let on what he'd found, the trees obliged them to move single-file.

Pat went ahead and, falling back, Campbell felt a cloud no bigger than his hand, but still a cloud, move over his mind as he watched Pat's shoulders lean to the grade, the lank of hair that spilled over his collar and the web of patches across his skinny butt.

He was something, all right—a bundle of worries and doubts and frets, a mind that stank like a mining camp privy, and a tongue that stung like a vinegarroon. Speak well of a thing or person, and Pat was sure to speak ill. Even speak well of him, and he'd likely turn it back on you with his own twist, or else seek hidden meanings. He was good at hidden meanings himself, and had his shadowy, unintended-seeming ways of reminding Campbell of his debt.

Coming down to it, Campbell thought, Pat was no more than a millstone around his neck, and he'd favor himself to get rid of him. Not that he hadn't thought of it more than once; but on the other hand, he also felt beholden to him and, if not grateful, at least inclined to overlook the worst in him, and even to feel sorry for him. Sometimes, in the deeps of his thoughts, he felt he put up with him by way of reaching backward to a cleaner time in his life—a kind of hair-shirt. But that wasn't clear by any means, and was only touched on while groping far back. Likely, it was just a habit. Or more to the point, and maybe truer, was that he feared Pat.

Maybe not, too; but it took the form of the little cloud that now lay on his thoughts. Five years of fending for Pat had got him so used to him that he'd almost lost sight of him as a man who might lean to a life that didn't depend on another.

Now, though, with Pat so owly lately, Campbell wondered if he mightn't be thinking of such. With money enough, he might, and could be he'd got wind of such. Could even be that he saw the same signs of a strike that Campbell himself had seen; and counting on that, might be feeling his oats while making plans of some kind.

That would explain it, he thought, and maybe would point to more. With money enough to be chief in his own tepee, Pat would have no further need of him and, in his spiteful way, might sell him out.

Just then, as the cloud threatened bigger size, they came out onto the edge of a meadow where a she-bear and two cubs frolicked and rolled about in the beds of harebell and yarrow and monkshood that lay in the middle like spilled paint. In the quiet air no scent carried, but now the horse sounds went out to them, and with a run of coughs and snorts, the she-bear cuffed her youngsters into a bumbling gallop toward the dark of the timber.

The sight made Campbell laugh, and the early mood came back, even as he held his horse against the wildness which its own sight of the bears had caused. He looked beyond Pat, who tilted and pitched and swore and sawed at the reins, and saw him for what he was—a weakling who did nothing well, a man who needed the crutch of another to bear him through life.

How could he ever fear a man like that? He could choke Pat's life out with one hand. He ought to be ashamed to think that Pat might dare sell him out.

The bear business over, Campbell rode easy and let his horse pick its way behind the others. They'd be near the top now, he thought, glancing up and around, and he wondered what Julius had in mind. Maybe a spring; he hoped it was. His day-old canteen water was stale and lukewarm.

For a moment he held his glance on Julius, seeing his beard go light and dark in sun and tree shadow; then he let it slide along the line, resting on each man in turn, until it came to Troy. There it stopped; the sight of him, together with the image of his own grass and water and stock, had put his mind upon Lilly. A place like he'd been thinking of all morning, and the new and different life that went with it, asked that a woman belong to it, too.

Now with his eye upon Troy, Lilly took shape in his mind, appearing in his sight at first as the girl he'd hardly looked at on coming to the Ross's; then the view passed to one of an evening in late spring, and to the vision of her changed from girl and far gone toward full womanhood.

Late afternoon of that day he'd been mending harness in the barn, alone. Julius was down at his shack, and Pat had gone to town hours before. It was hot in the barn, and after a snooze in the hay, he went to the loft for a pull at a bottle that he'd hid from Pat. It was there he'd heard splashing, and looking through a crack between the boards, saw Lilly as naked as when born, bathing in the cattle tank.

Hardly daring to breathe, he watched her from the time the sunlight made of her a smooth and shining white otter, until dusk had turned her skin to gold in the afterglow. She swam about in the shallow water, and sang. She lay on her back with her arms spread and her young breasts curving upward to the changing sky, her slender body tapered to her waist, and her legs, below the dark wedge of her groin, going from sight in the shaded water. A dove planed down and circled and hooed, and she waved and hooed back. Once a young bull came to drink, and when it finished, she ran laughing and splashing toward it and put it to flight.

Something about the sight so filled and swelled his throat that he could scarce swallow.

He watched for half an hour, and when at last she'd dried herself and, wrapped in her old dress, gone slowly up to the house, he had the feeling of having been through something hard to name, but that came back to him whenever he thought of that time.

It was with him now as he climbed the last of this mountain. She was woman enough for any man, and with money to set up on his own, there'd be small trouble from old Matt. True, Merril seemed to have ideas, but he was no more knowing than a puppy, and could easily be fixed.

All at once he felt the grade ease, and under him the earth became level. Beyond, Julius called, "Hold up, now!" Coming out of his dream, Campbell slowed to a halt among the others.

They stood in a group on what seemed to be the edge of the world. Almost at their feet the mountain fell off nearly sheer into a valley way lower than Lonesome Valley. Through it flowed a river that caught the sun's flash, where cottonwood trees stood high and full-crowned. Beyond, grass deepened toward rimrock, ridging out shelf on shelf into more grass, and giving way in time to a rolling redearth country mottled in green fists of cedar and piñon and juniper. This in its time beached against a wall of reaching cliffs, as red as blood and deep in forests of blue pine, and at a great distance crowned by a single mountain of three sharp peaks.

If only from hearsay, Campbell knew where he was. The cliffs were part of the Mogollon Rim, and the mountain above, the San Francisco Peaks. In all of the thousand square miles of land that he could see, there was none that he had ever heard of holding gold.

"That there's the Verde down there," Old Man Harper was saying. He pointed with his hand, and his beard pointed, too. "Yonder's where we're going. No reason you shouldn't know now."

Campbell turned. "Where?" he said.

"There's canyons in the Rim that ought to hold something."

"The *Rim?*" Campbell said, and his voice sounded strange. He stared out at the crimson walls, wondering if he'd heard right.

"You're looking at it," Julius said. "That country ain't never been touched at all."

Campbell believed it then; he didn't wonder that it never had been touched. "Why, you damned old fool!" he blazed up. "That's sandstone country! Whoever heard of gold ore showing in sandstone?"

Julius's voice was still quiet, but honed to an edge. "The Rim is capped with lava there. Where lava shows, there's bound to be dikes and chimneys."

"So that's it! We're going to hunt needles in haystacks!"

"Feel free to leave at any time," Julius said, his tone mocking, but holding at the same time a hint of danger if pushed too far. "Just remember that I didn't guarantee no gold; only a place to look for it."

Campbell had to laugh now, but laughter without humor. It all fit together now so well. What he'd seen in Julius as the silence of knowing was really the silence of leading them on until too late to turn back. Even the little mystery that he'd made of the Tucson road pointed that way. With all of his talk and tales, Julius was only a pocket-hunter chasing a gold mirage. Only a fool would think otherwise now.

Campbell laughed again; and then the laugh choked off. He felt cheated and let down, and nothing whatever remained of the good day. He might never have shot his deer, or walked alone in the quiet forest, or thought what he had of what might come.

He looked around him; the others stared off, maybe not yet understanding. Well, all right, he thought. Let it be so then. He'd been pleased enough to think of it as share and share alike in what might be found, but it was different now with only hen-feed or worse in prospect. It was bad enough to be made a fool of once; he wouldn't allow it to happen again. He'd keep a sharp eye out for number one.

Ahead of him, as they made their way toward what turned out to be a little seep after all, he heard Pat laughing in high good humor; but Campbell was too deep down in dark thoughts to wonder why.

CHAPTER EIGHT

Ash stepped out of the lean-to into the early light of the day, and for a moment stood sniffing the piñon scent, looking about and listening. On the east the ragged faces of cliffs rising two or three thousand feet were still in deep shadow, though on top, on the Rim, the mat of pine and spruce and hemlock rose sharp and clear with dawn swelling behind it. On the west, where sunlight was just touching, the walls were colored in bands of red and cream, and with knots of green that were small trees and bushes growing from seams. The big trees on top were clear, too, but as the sky behind them was still dull, they didn't stand out like those on the other side. Over his head the sky had gone a mourning dove color.

He stood sniffing and looking and listening, while he wondered where Shep could be. Shep had been away all night long again. Living on red meat, and with all of nature to wander in, he was getting to be a case.

Going on so for long, he might even take up with a coyote or wolf one day; if he didn't get killed first.

The notion moved him to whistle; and with his fingers to his mouth, he cut loose a shiver of sound that bounded from the cliffs, then funneled up into the canyon mouth in a shriek of echoes.

There was no reply to this from Shep; but one came from the lean-to where Troy and Campbell and McGuire were beginning to stir about.

"Good Christ!" Pat yelled. "D'you have to do that?"

"I'm just calling Shep," Ashley answered.

"That beast is worse away than around," Pat said.

"Time to be about another work day, anyhow. Them as work."

"Smart kid," Pat said; then his voice took on its tone of being picked on. "Any time you want my twisted ankle, you're welcome."

Having his doubts about Pat's ankle, Ashley didn't answer that time. He moved away to the creek that was talking away in its bed beyond the lean-to. Cupping the water into his hands, he splashed it over his face and neck, feeling his wind catch and the blood race in his skin. It was colder than you'd think for this time of year, icy even. But then Julius said that springs, far up-canyon, fed it, and so it didn't change much with the seasons.

The washing done, he wiped his face on his shirtsleeve while he gazed across the placer diggings into the dark canyon mouth. Somewhere up in the deep, shadowy heart was Julius, he thought, still looking for dikes and chimneys. Unless he'd found one and started back down, maybe with news of a paying vein. Ever since getting here he'd spent most of his time up there, searching, coming down only once every week or ten days for supplies.

Thinking of it, looking into the squeeze of cliffs at the mouth, Ash wished that he might go himself sometime, to see what things were like way up there. But he hadn't so far, and no one else had either. Julius always said there wasn't any point in such until he found something worthwhile; then they'd break camp and all go up. Meantime, he said, it was best to work the placer down here. It paid somewhat.

Well, maybe he was right, and now the day's digging was in Ash's mind. He headed back to the lean-to. On the way he stopped at the sprawling tangle of branches dragged in at the end of a rope by Jack and Pat—mostly fallen juniper and piñon, but here and there also a piece of incense cedar, that smelled good in a fire but spit too much. A few times he'd mentioned that, but still they brought it, maybe not caring. They didn't do much cutting or sawing either, and even looked on dragging it in as a favor.

He took a few odd lengths that would do for breakfast, and went to the lean-to. The others were up now, humping around in the half-light, going outdoors to wash and water out. Only Pat lay in his blankets still, as if to show that his ankle was worse than doubters might think.

"You know, kid," he said, resting easy while Ash kindled a fire, "I'd help in a minute if I could. Old leg got me hog-tied, though."

Near a week ago, Pat had caught his foot in a seam. Some days it was good, others bad. Ordinarily it was worse when there was work on hand.

"Lots of leg-work building a fire," Ash said, fanning the flicker of flame in the small stuff.

"It's the hunching around," Pat said. "I could easy lose my balance and fall in."

A treat, Ash thought; but didn't say it. He only snorted, while he fed some branches in. He pulled the coffeepot over. "Being careful, you might pass that tow sack without danger," he said.

McGuire managed this, taking it down from a knob in the log wall behind him, where it was kept by night against prowling animals. By day it hung on the branch of an oak outdoors. In it were grease in a can, left-over biscuits and odds and ends of deer meat. With Julius there, they had Dutch oven cooking even for breakfast; but it changed with him gone. Then they ate from the sack and only cooked in the evening.

When Troy and Jack came back, the coffee was hot. Ash poured it into the tin cups on the hearthstone, and opened the sack. He took what he wanted, leaving the sack on the dirt floor in reach of the others.

"I swear," Troy said, while he sipped at his cup, "this ain't bad. You're near as good as a woman, Ash."

With his mouth full of biscuit, Ash could only grunt; but it was just as well anyway. He'd noticed the little ways that Troy used in making up to him for blowing up when the burro died, and he felt wary.

But if he couldn't speak himself, a man could always count on Pat to stick his nose in.

"As good as a woman in certain departments, you mean," he said.

"Well, sure, there's some he wouldn't shine at," Troy said.

Campbell looked at Ash. "Wouldn't be fair, though, to expect a kid to know about them. Unless he knows more'n we think he does."

Catching Jack's glance, Ashley was reminded of another such—three months ago, when Lilly had appeared with the bucket. But maybe it wasn't the same kind at all; and anyhow, Pat was going again.

"Woman or no," he said, as if Ash were absent, "I do wish he'd fire up that Dutch oven mornings. Julius don't stick us with old biscuits."

As with building the fire, the first man up and around made breakfast, too. It never came to much, but Ashley couldn't help but notice how often it fell to him. Try as he might, he never could wait the others out. He always had to see what the new morning looked like.

"I guess you know what you can do about that," Ash told him.

"Don't get me wrong, boy. I ain't complaining, just wishing."

"Well, you can wish yourself to getting breakfast, then. I won't stop you. You can fire up the Dutch oven, too."

But Pat was no longer thinking of the Dutch oven, or of breakfast, either. The talk had passed to Julius, speculating on his whereabouts and when he'd show again. It was getting to be like any other morning in the past eight weeks: the rolling out of their blankets, the little needling while they wakened fully and got food into them. Soon enough they'd be about whatever they had to do, but first there was coffee and talk.

"Wherever he is, he'd better find something soon," Troy said.

"Aye to that," Pat said. "Snowtime ain't far, not here, anyhow."

"I remember when you liked the thought of snow," Campbell said.

"Like hell," Pat said; then, as if there might be room for doubt, he said, "Anyway, I don't remember it."

"I do," Jack said. "Back at Matt's place, on a hot summer day. You was butted up to a cottonwood log."

There was no reason for Ash to be surprised that Jack remembered. He remembered himself now that it came up. What surprised him was Jack's sureness, as if all about the journey was kept in his mind, as in a book.

Somehow it made him uneasy, and as he looked at Jack he saw that Troy and McGuire were also watchful.

Then Jack laughed, as though it didn't come to anything; and perhaps it didn't. "I don't think snowtime's going to make any difference," he said.

"How so?" Troy asked.

"Just what I said. Snow or otherwise, I don't see us going back any different than we came."

"Richer, you mean," Pat put in. "We'll go back older; that's different," and he laughed, but stopped when no one else laughed.

"Well, older, but no more than that," Campbell said.

"Don't forget that two hundred dollars from the placer," Ash said.

Jack gave Ash a glance. "In eight weeks, and split five ways." He raised his cup and drank, as if more words were needless; but then he said, "I doubt he'll find gold enough up there to fill a tooth."

"What about the placer gold?" Ash said. "It come from somewhere."

"It could come from anywhere," Jack said. "The lode could be a hundred miles off. More maybe. It wouldn't surprise me any to learn he's only fishing or lying around in the sun. How do we know?"

More and more, lately, Campbell had been going on so —beginning with his flare-up at Julius in the Black Hills. The moment, or its memory, seemed to color all he'd said and done, or hadn't said and done, since.

Still, it didn't seem right to Ash that Julius should be picked apart while not around to get a word in.

"You got to give him time," Ash said. "It takes a lot of drilling and digging and poking around."

"No need to tell us how time passes," Pat McGuire said. "We know."

"All the time in the world won't help him," Jack said, and paused and lit a cigarette he'd rolled. "It just ain't there."

"How do you know?" Ash said. "Julius don't figure that way."

"He's a crazy old man, kid," Campbell said. "Can't you tell yet?"

"Well, my God, he wouldn't bring us all the way up here for nothing, would he? If he *knew* there wasn't anything, I mean."

Jack got settled on his heels and flicked an ash from his smoke. "Listen, kid, don't be so simple. You heard his tales, ain't you?"

"Sure, I heard 'em. So what?"

"All about the Lost Tayopa and the Lost Adams and the Lost Six-Shooter and the Lost Mexican Ledge and the Lost Old Woman..."

"All right, I heard 'em," Ash said. "What about 'em?"

"Well, they all got one thing in common, one thing in each one the same as all the others. They're lost, and can't be found. That's what."

Campbell's manner was like a preacher giving his views on a revelation, and when he finished no one spoke right away; he blew a smoke ring out, and everyone watched him run his finger through it.

Then he said, "What d'you think of that?"

"By God, that's so!" Troy said in a breath.

"You're damned right it's so," Jack said. "We got the same thing right here; he's drawn to that kind. He can't help himself."

"All we need for this one is a name," Pat said, grinning like he'd seen it in the same way, and his pleasure with his wisdom was too big to let himself be put out with the meaning of it.

Ashley couldn't tell if they believed that or not—it had all the earmarks of an alibi for sloping off work. But he wouldn't let himself believe it—not yet, anyhow. They'd put too much in this trip; at least, he had. And it didn't add up anyhow. No one could be so crazy.

"You can't expect him to find the right formation straight off," he said all at once. "Say he finds a dike that looks good— maybe andesite. Say it's iron-stained, too. All right. First off, then, he's got to figure how to get at it. That takes time. Then, decided, he's got to go in a certain ways to get a fair sample. That takes more time. Say, then, the dike is full of rotten quartz that makes it look good, and keeps him digging. Only it isn't any good at all. But it takes awhile to find that out. Time he does, a week goes by, maybe more. Then, knowing that, he's got to pull out and start all over, hunting more andesite, or rhyolite or phonolite or latite or whatever."

For Ashley, it was like a speech, and when he stopped everyone listened and watched as they had when Jack had put his finger through the smoke ring. Only now, they watched *him*.

"Well, Jeezaws," Troy said finally, "listen to that!"

"Ain't he something?" Pat said. "A regular Cousin-Jack."

"Where'd you pick that up?" Campbell said, and now there seemed to be something careful in the way he watched Ashley.

"Why, from Julius," Ash said. "Where else?"

"When?" Jack Campbell asked.

"When...?" and Ashley tried to think when; but he was thinking more of a reason for them to be surprised. There was none for it, yet they were. "Why, all along, I guess. He's been talking that way enough. You only got to listen."

"You ever been around the mines?" Jack said. "Tombstone? Bisbee?"

"Me?" Ash said. "No, I never been around any mines."

"What about Silver City?" Pat asked; then, it seemed to Ash, that on a glance from Campbell, Pat drew in.

"There, neither," Ash said, and now he felt his face redden and his neck grow stiff. They made it seem wrong that he listen to Julius, rather than ridicule or doubt him. "What's that got to do with it?"

"Nothing, I guess," Jack said. "Maybe Julius ain't so crazy as we think; maybe he ain't just fishing."

"Not that we can tell either way," Troy said. "Seeing that he wants us all to stay here, waiting."

"That could be fixed," Campbell said, "easy enough."

He began to rise, and McGuire leaned toward Ash. "What else he have to say about it, kid?"

"Julius?" Ash said. "About what?"

"About up there, where he's been? What'd he tell you?"

"Nothing, goddam it! It's only talk, that's all." Troy was up now, and Ash rose, too. He looked down at Pat. "You'd hear it, too, if you wasn't talkin' so much yourself."

"Unless he was only telling you, hey?"

"I said," Ash began; but then he stopped, not going on. He was tired of hearing of it. He reached for his cup and dropped it into the pan against washing. He took his ducking jacket from his bedroll and stepped outside. He turned to call Troy, but Jack had come out behind him with his rifle; he was ready for hunting, and all at once Ash would like to go, too. The dismal start of the day made him want to get far away from camp.

"How about it, Jack? How about taking me?"

"Best you stay and dig, kid," Campbell said. "Only need one hunting for a few days. Still got a quarter hanging."

"Maybe you could help dig, then, if we've got so much hanging."

"Oh, we ain't got that much." Jack grinned. "And anyhow, I got to keep on learning the country. May pay off some day."

Ash could be wrong, but it seemed to him that Pat McGuire roused on that point. Anyhow he called from inside. "Hold on, Jack; lemme drag myself to a horse and come along."

"Nothing doing," Campbell said. "You ain't fit to ride."

"Hell, I'm all right once I'm up."

"Nothing doing. I'd spend the day fishing you out of thickets."

He started moving off, as though to get away from more of Pat's arguments; but then a thought took hold of him, and he turned about and stepped close to Ashley. He was grinning when he said, "I don't think you'd hold out on us, would you, Merril?"

"What?" Ash said, and he wondered what was meant. The change in thought had been too quick. Then he knew what Jack meant, but Jack was going on again.

"I wouldn't do that, if I was you," he said to Ashley, and Ashley heard him very clearly. "Never, never would I do that, not in a million years."

CHAPTER NINE

When Troy came out of the lean-to, Ashley and he put the tools on their horses and set off for the placer diggings half a mile upstream. Arriving, they unloaded, and Ash began to shovel sand into the rocker box while Troy put the horses on picket.

The days were still warm enough, Ash thought; but now at the end of October the nights ran cold, and until such time in the morning that work at the rocker had got his blood moving, his jacket felt good. True, they couldn't yet see much color on the Rim, but then there wasn't much growth that changed on the cliffs that overlooked camp and the canyon mouth anyway: some sumac gone red, a few touches of maple, and a fringe of rusty fern along the edge. But that about summed it up. No aspen grew nearby, and all else was some kind of evergreen.

Still, fall was hard on them. Out in the rolling red-earth land among the crimson monuments that stood away from the Rim, the piñon nuts were tasty. The deer were all in the blue now, and the bucks well antlered. The air was quiet, as it often was while winter gathered itself, and only yesterday a wedge of geese had gone over, heading south.

Around camp, and up on the bar where they worked, there were other signs, too. A good many song-birds were gone—vireos and tanagers and certain thrashers, bright-looking birds that seemed to need the brightest sun to live in. The grass was whiter and drier, and easily trampled to dust underfoot. In camp they'd pulled down the tarps that had served as a tent for August and September, and made a lean-to out of logs closed on three sides, with a fireplace and chimney. The third side could be closed, too, if need be, against bad weather or the sudden onset of winter.

Of course, they'd be gone by winter; but even so it was a sign of the new season.

For a moment the thought of that, along with the time spent here so far, made Ash straighten and look toward camp. The lean-to stood under a sycamore tree whose trunk showed through its patchy, tattered bark like bone. The woodpile sprawled at one side, and the venison hung from an oak near it. At a distance, grazing on bottomland grass, a few horses showed.

All, he guessed, was a measure of the time passed here since coming down from the Black Hills. But a truer measure of that time, and of the work done in it, was in the placer diggings that filled every square foot of the way between camp and where they now worked. The rounded humps of gravel and sand stood solid in rows along both sides of the creek. Above these there spread out on the talus slopes of the cliffs countless upside-down Vees made of holes from which the earth had been dug and washed in the rocker with water brought down in the flume that took it from the creek at a little falls up above. The points of the Vees showed where the gold, usually no more than a hint of color, had died out, and the tailing piles were what was left. Each time a new Vee was dug, the flume would have to be torn apart and moved upstream. Then in another few days the whole thing would have to be done over again.

To show for eight weeks of digging and rocking and washing and piling and building and rebuilding the flume, there was under the hearthstone of the lean-to about two hundred and twenty dollars in recovered free gold.

No matter that Ashley's hands were as hard as horn now, and his shoulders felt able to bear an ox yoke, he would call a man who held gold-mining an easy way to riches, stark, staring mad.

Still, he didn't mind too much; you never knew what you could do until you got at it. At least he liked it better than Troy, and a lot better than Pat and Jack. Julius didn't count, as he was gone so much, hunting the big bonanza that would make it all worthwhile.

❧ ❧ ❧

Ash raised up a shovel of sand to the rocker that, along with the flume, they'd knocked together of green boards whipsawed from pine, and then Troy let the handle fall idle.

"I wonder when Julius will show," he said, as if a part of Ash's thought had got to him now. "Been gone eight days this time; be eight by evening."

"Don't start on that again," Ash said. "I've had my fill for one day." He raised another load into the rocker. "He'll come when he's good and ready."

But having started, Troy kept on; though not yet along the line that Jack and Pat had taken.

"Maybe he's lost. Or maybe the Indians got him."

"He couldn't get lost in a canyon. And I doubt there's Indians about, saving those that built the ruins around in the cliffs. And they're long dead."

"Don't fool yourself," Troy said. "This country's full of 'em. Been plenty Apaches through here, I'll bet. And Navajo land is north only a few days."

"Maybe, but still we've seen no sign of any."

Ash finished filling the rocker; then he waited for Troy to move the handle. But Julius had got in the way of Troy's moving the handle, and he was looking north, as if expecting he might catch sight of Julius.

"I wonder if they're right," he said, and Ashley knew that Troy had come to Campbell's view, after all. "Maybe he knows more'n he's told. Maybe he's even onto something up there."

Then Troy's eye came sliding to Ashley, maybe wondering what *he* might know, and Ash felt his head grow hot; then he felt an urge to laugh. Then he just felt disgusted.

"Those two," he said. "They whine and cry because they ain't rich yet. But let Julius try to make them rich, and they're suspicious."

"I'm just saying it could be," Troy said. "And that's all they said, too. It's natural to think that with him gone so much."

"It depends on who's thinking," Ash said.

"Even so, it'd be better if he showed more often. He could help with this, too. We could use some help, I'm thinking."

"My God," Ash said, "the more time he spends here, the less he has for hunting chimneys!"

"We could use some help from him though," Troy said, still holding on. "It's poor doings digging like this all day long."

"Coming to that, we could use some from Pat and Jack," Ash said.

That was different, of course, and Troy was straight away full of reminders of the difference. "Now you know the agreement says they're to do the hunting."

"It's always seemed more like an announcement to me," Ash said. "And, anyhow, I figured that was only while coming up here."

"Don't we need meat right along?" Troy said. "Besides they do help now and then. But with Pat down only Jack can hunt now."

"I ain't talking about just now," Ash said. "I'm talking about in general. They could easy pitch in a whole lot more'n they do. Splitting five ways what us two find don't seem fair somehow."

Troy didn't say how fair he thought it was; in fact, he said nothing, and fell to moving the rocker handle. Still, now that it had come up, it nagged at Ash; and after a time of watching the water sluice through the box, he turned his glance toward camp below.

The sight of a trickle of smoke rising up from the stick and mud chimney made it nag more; he'd killed the fire when they'd left.

"Pat don't seem too lame to hobble to the coffeepot," he said. "Having him out of business is like having an extra mouth to feed."

With Ashley's voice lifted to be heard above the rocker and water, Troy let fall the handle again, and looked south himself.

"Maybe we ought to get *him* out here to work that handle," Ash half yelled. "That takes no leg-work. You could shovel then, too."

Troy stepped away from the rocker altogether.

"I wouldn't talk so loud, if I was you, Ash Merril. These canyon walls carry sound easy. He just might hear you."

"So what if he does?" Ash said.

"I'd just be careful how I talked about him, that's all," Troy said. "And Campbell, too. Maybe they ain't all you think they are."

"And I suppose you know better."

"I know enough," Troy said, and drew up, as if the meaning of what he knew put him on higher ground than what Ash stood on.

"For all of me, they're just a couple of range bums," Ash said, though he wasn't so sure of this any longer. His ideas had undergone a change, especially toward Jack. But he wouldn't let Troy know that.

Saying what he did, however, brought a new expression to Troy's face, one that might be worn by a man who carried a handful of eggs across bad ground.

"Goddam it, Ash, you be careful. More'n one wise kid's dug his grave with his own tongue."

"You're likely right," Ash said. "You know so much."

With little dents at the corners of his mouth, Troy's voice turned softer. "I'm only warning you; don't forget, I'm responsible for you."

Ashley put the blade of the shovel into the tailing pile. "I'm damned if you are; you're hardly responsible for yourself."

"I'm warning you all the same," Troy said, while the dents grew deeper. "I wouldn't be no friend of yours otherwise."

Ashley shoved the blade in deeper and laughed. Then he felt an urge to put his hand in Troy's face and dump him into the rocker. Troy should speak of friendship after standing idle when the burro was swept away. With all of Troy's put-on, his preaching over what he knew in secret, the memory fanned up hot and swift. "Some friend you are! Time to show it, and you back down!"

Troy's voice went up a note now, showing that he knew what Ash meant, though it hadn't been named. "Goddam it, you didn't ask for no help!"

"I said once, I didn't think I had to!" Ash said, his own voice lifting higher.

"I didn't aim to stick my nose in, unasked!"

"You don't need to tell me!"

"That damned beast wouldn't have made it anyway!" Troy shouted. "Letting it go was a kindness; it was quick and simple!"

"What's that got to do with it?" Ash came back—though he'd nearly come to that point himself. But that didn't matter now. "You only aimed to do what Campbell and McGuire did—plain nothing!"

"That's a goddammed lie!" Troy yelled.

His face was dead white now, his body trembling. Ash had seen him mad at other times, but never like this—not even when Ash had climbed to high ground from the wash. No doubt the tying of his failing to Pat and Jack did it; but Ash didn't care. He plowed on, pushed and spurred by all the feeling that was bottled up inside since that day.

"It ain't a lie!" he yelled back. "You'd rather be dead than do different than them!"

That was too much for Troy. He threw his arm back to swing. Coming forward in a wild loop, the blind force got his legs snarled in the shovel before him; not even looking, he grabbed it for support, and when he straightened, his hands still held onto it. Now he swung *it* back, and Ash threw up his arms and shouted, "Troy!" But Troy's face was blank. The blade began to sweep ahead, and Ash yelled, "Troy!" again, but Troy was deaf, too.

Then he yelled again, as hard as he could, and that time got through. Troy stopped the flying blade in mid-air. Maybe knowing for the first time what he held, he stared a long time at it, then at Ash, too, while his color came back and his breath shook in and out.

Then, as *something* must be done with it, he ducked his eyes from Ashley's sight and began filling the rocker.

Troy did all the shovel work for the rest of that day. Since he shied away from such as a rule, Ashley knew that he ought to take some pleasure in it. But he didn't. He was far too low in his mind for pleasure of any kind.

They'd quarreled a good deal before now, him and Troy, and fought a few times, too—mostly with Ashley losing; but he'd never until now seen what looked like murder in Troy's face.

CHAPTER TEN

Pretty soon, Julius figured, he'd have to break his camp and go down and tell the others. But there was no real hurry yet. He still had time.

He lay in the shallows of the creek, his beard floating on the water like a beaver's tail. Underneath he felt the red stone of the shelf against his bony hips, and the warmth of the sun coming down on his face and reflecting from the scarlet walls of the narrow side canyon. The water was cold, though, being shallow and slower than the main creek, it could be worse; and anyhow he took pride in standing up to it. Few men of his age could stay long in water that made you numb all over, and it pleased him that he still could.

He let his head go farther back, and for a time looked overhead. In the way of box canyons, the walls rose sheer, and pressed close against the creek. Wandering into this place a number of days back, after scouting the main canyon for ten or more miles above the lean-to over a time of eight weeks, he'd come with small hope. There was almost no talus slope, and he'd been doubtful of spending any time up here. It surely didn't look like gold-bearing country, even less than in the main canyon. The bed of the creek was all rock, with hardly a show of sand and gravel.

But then he'd found that one bar; and pointing upward from it in a long, slender finger, the talus slope that reached directly into a narrow, hidden crevice in the soaring cliffs. And there the great dike rose, glinting and shining so with hair-thin golden wires that he'd broken down and wept openly at first sight of it.

So, it was true, after all; no matter the country-rock, gold was still where you happened to find it.

Taking his hands from the shelf, he let the easy current work at his body. Like an old log, he turned slowly, and when his eyes came around in line with the crevice some thirty yards upstream of where he lay, he stopped. Then he waved with one hand.

"Hi, there, Mr. Chimney!" he shouted. "I tracked you down at last, you son-of-a-bitch!"

High above, a piñon jay flew squawking from a skinny lodgepole pine that grew from the cliff, and made for the Rim. Off to the side, a bushy tailed squirrel froze stone-still to a ledge and stared down, pop-eyed. The sound swelled and squeezed along through the narrow walls, echoing at each turn, until it might have been ten men shouting.

It even startled him, and for a space he thought, "Great Jesus, they'll hear me all the way to the lean-to!" Then he thought, "No, they won't—too far. But, what of it? It's theirs, too, ain't it?"

So, he shouted again, "Hi, there, Mr. Chimney! I tracked you down at last, you son-of-a-bitch!"

Now for a while he simply sprawled in the sunshine like a riverboat on a mud bank. He let his eyes laze up the talus finger to the crevice, then brought them down. He did this several times, letting them pause each trip a little longer at the top, teasing himself. Then when he could no longer stand it, he closed his eyes and sent his mind on through the crevice entrance to behold the lode.

Now in the water his fingers moved, as his thoughts moved them over the surface of quartz. He felt his eyelids twitch as the eyeballs swung and raised and lowered to gauge his wealth.

How long a wait had it been? Seventy-one now, he'd been thirty-six on heading for Placerville and Oroville in 1850; thirty-five years since going to California. Half his life almost, and seeming more when he considered all the other names that fell between then and now: Downieville, Mariposa City, Agua Fria,

Virginia City, Pike's Peak, Central City, La Paz and Ehrenburg, the Vulture and the old Silver King. A mapful of names that covered the country from the Rockies to the Pacific. And all the names of places that were on no map; and all the places without names that were only a shape and form in the mind, but places still, and helped fill the stretch of years running in his thoughts.

Well, it was a time, all right, a right smart time of waiting and hoping, and of believing in order to bear the waiting until now.

But it was worth it. At least it was if he could make a decent guess on first sight. Roughly, there might be a hundred thousand dollars in that chimney, maybe more depending on depth and width. Of course there'd be no telling until he made his entry and set to drilling and stoping. Veins varied in their value; a spadeful at one point could be worth ten at another, only a foot away. Then, too, the vein could pinch out; instead of a simple fissure vein, it could easily turn out as a fault fissure vein. A heap of difference there.

The thought of that difference roused him now. He opened his eyes and squinted at the crevice. If a simple fissure yielded a hundred thousand, a fault fissure could skin that to fifty. And if the fault began right underfoot, or in the ceiling right overhead, it could be even less. The chance made him angry, and he heaved up on his elbows.

"You miserable bastard!" he shouted. "You planning to pinch me out? Don't you dare! I've used up half my life tracking you down!"

Then as the echo came back upon him like an army shouting, he felt shamed. Rather than angry, he should be grateful for whatever the dike held. And even if it did pinch out, the wealth gained would still be far and above what most miners found in a life of hunting it. Fifty thousand dollars wasn't to be sneezed at.

"It's all right, Pet!" he called out. "I didn't mean that! You just go on being what you are!"

Now he felt better, and lay at ease again in the water, closing his eyes and spreading out upon the sun-warmed shelf. He relaxed, feeling the little nudgings of the creek, until there came a point where he no longer seemed a thinking, planning human from the outside, but some feeling part of the wild, aware and knowing, and answering its currents.

This, he thought, as from a great way, was the best time of all; the pause and rest that followed the triumph, the moment of tasting victory over the luckless, wandering effort of so many years. It was that special and rare instant when he held the great bonanza in his hand; but was not yet obliged to consider the labor and hazards in removing and keeping it. He wasn't even yet thinking of ways to spend it; he was simply savoring it. It was that kind of time.

Had he been a Navajo who, by mistake or otherwise, had made the perfect blanket, he might even think of it as the right time to die.

When he opened his eyes again, the sun had moved west. It was still on his face but no longer fell so directly on the shelf. An hour and more might have passed while he lay there, unknowing. It made him wonder if he'd slept; but he doubted it. Likely the pleasure of his thoughts had just idled his mind against all else.

Now, however, he was well aware of the cold of the water, and he pushed himself up on his butt. Standing, he rubbed his body with his hands, and then stepped to dry rock, where he stood in the full warmth of the sun.

It was noon, he guessed, squinting up, and he'd better start heading back. He'd been gone nine days this time, nine and a half to be exact, and they'd be wondering where he was. Leaving now and getting in at early dark would make ten. They'd be wondering, all right.

He raised his eyes and looked above at the crevice, now in shadow, secret and yet promising, something like a woman that he might have known when younger, and that he now hated to leave. But he had no choice about that; ten days would have them plenty antsy down below; they might even be on the point of looking for him.

"Don't get lonely, Pet!" he called. "I'm only going down to tell the others about you! We'll all be back in a few days!"

Then a frown came into his mind. It was the first time he'd put the lode and "them" together into spoken words, and he wasn't sure that he liked the sound of it.

But then, why shouldn't they know? Why else set out together on this search? It wasn't no berry-picking party.

Leaning on a rock, he started pulling on his long-handled underwear. His legs in, he stood away to work his arms through the holes, then he made sure of the button that closed the gap in back, and reached for his trousers.

His mind was on the work now. First thing, they'd have to move camp. That would take a couple of days, considering all the gear; then they'd have to rig another lean-to, cut and drag the logs down from above, and all else that went with it; unless they knocked the old one down and packed it up. In the long run, time might be saved by so doing.

Well, it was a detail right now; and with his shirt on, he pushed his feet into his brogans while he looked along the wall where the crevice lay. That was where the real work would be; all else, the moving, building a new lean-to, were only means to an end.

And there'd be plenty to do before they could make the most of the vein's worth. Alone, a pick-ax and a dozen powder charges would set him on easy street. But nothing so crude as that would make a killing for five men. There'd have to be some real hard-rock mining before a crowd of that size made out.

The crevice, no doubt, was the place to start, he thought as he drew up his laces. One man had a kind of squeeze getting in there, let alone have working space for more. Widened, it would be all right, and the rock removed would make the talus slope more solid, too. They'd need a head-frame from which to string ropes for buckets, and they could only rig it on pilings sunk in the talus. Then, when ready to take out ore, they'd need an *arrastre* to grind it in. That, too, they'd have to build of what lay at hand, and have to run it on horsepower.

His boots tied, he stood up, and with the *arrastre* still in mind, looked about for a decent place where they could build it—a flat one, not too far from the slope, was best. Right where he was standing wasn't bad, though narrow. Across the water from him, there looked to be another, maybe better. One or two others also showed up, but they were too choked in brush and rockfall to come to anything.

It was one of these, however, that held his eye the longest, and put a new thought in his head. This particular hollow in the cliff was dense in grass, about the only good stand he'd seen in here. But it would never do for nine horses; and otherwise, only scattered browse cropped up along the ledges—what his own horse had fed on. That meant a forage problem; grass would have to be cut and hauled from the main canyon.

But there was more to it than that. The grass was brown, dead now with fall. Up here in the deep, narrow canyon heart, the winterkill would come earlier than down below at the mouth where they had camp.

Reading the message of the dead grass, he knew that it was all a matter of time: time to move camp and rebuild here; time to get the crevice entered and build the head-frame; time to clear ground for the *arrastre*; time to cut grass. Even with five men, a month of effort would pass before they could remove ore. By then the country could be under its first snow; sooner, if winter was early. And it could easily be buried deep by the time the lode was paying.

He swung his foot and sent a stone into the water, but his eye held on the brown, dead grass; then he moved it slowly to the cliff, where in seams and cracks, sumac flamed in scarlet shoals. Higher, random maple burned in lone bursts of fire on the ledges and in far, cleaving draws; and on the very edge of the Rim, at the end of his sight, high, thin aspens set their ivory trunks and trembling, gold-coin leaves against the blue sky.

No one but a blind man could doubt that winter was on the march, and maybe a blind man wouldn't doubt.

It was damned peculiar how you missed things sometimes, he thought. It must have been his excitement over the find. Lying around here for three days in simple-headed pleasure had closed his mind to all else.

Well, he'd finished daydreaming now. Winter was a cold, looming fact. There was time to build the works, and make a start on mining, but that was all. Winter would then have them, and would drive them out until spring; and meantime there was the chance of some wanderer finding it. The headframe would tell; then there'd be trouble.

Walking along the ledge toward the talus slope, he wondered now if it wasn't better to delay things. Might be best to let the lode lie fallow through winter; then they'd have all of next spring and summer and fall to make the most of it.

But there was still the danger of some sharp-eyed person stumbling onto it. Hadn't he? And as to filing, a claim had never been known to keep jumpers away. To file in country where gold was unknown would simply draw attention.

That brought him to a still bigger danger. To think of "them" knowing of the lode had made his mind frown before, and now the frown grew. It would be bad to have "them" winter in the south with that knowledge. "They" might scheme up ways to cut him out. It might be wiser to keep his mouth shut.

Just then he reached the foot of the slope and, looking up, saw the crevice sixty or seventy feet above. From below an idle glance might take it as shadow or a dark stain of seepage. But it was still a cleavage, caused, likely, by heat and pressure of the chimney bulging up through the sandstone.

A knowing man might guess, just as he had.

He stood there, held in place by all these new and dark thoughts. In his mind the frown had turned to a black scowl. He ought to be getting on, he told himself; but all at once, he wanted a last look at the lode. Another look might help him decide what to say in camp.

"Hey, there, Pet!" he called out. "I'm coming up for a good-by kiss! Get ready!"

He climbed, hauling and pulling himself, scrabbling with his hands from grip to grip. Ground to small, loose stone and flowing sand by time and weather, the slope was hard going. It always took him four or five minutes to make his way up; he was blowing when he reached it.

It was different, though, once in. He forgot his weariness and the dark, scowling thoughts that nagged him. There in the trickle of light from outside, the golden wires glinted, putting all else from his mind.

"By Jesus, Pet," he said, "what a living beauty you are!"

Then, until his wind returned, he leaned against the wall and let his eyes feast. They were used to the dimness by now and could make out all of the glitter in such of the dike that showed from floor to ceiling—around six or seven feet. Also, in a moment or so, they could make out his powder keg and drills, his coil of fuse and hammer and pick-ax, stored beside one wall against return.

My God, he thought, how he'd like to stay here, and not have to come back.

A kind of trembling, as of sudden cold, took hold of him, and then, before he knew it, he seized the pick and drove it ringing into the face of the vein. A piece of rock sprang out on the floor, and he picked it up and took it into clear light. It was pure rose quartz, stitched and webbed with gold wire.

"Goddam it, you could pack a million in your guts!" he shouted.

Then he calmed down. The vein would have to be extremely deep, and rise extremely high, to hold that. The chance of faulting crossed his mind again, too. Any figuring had to allow for that.

He studied the face of the vein while he put the piece of quartz away in a little buckskin sack that hung at his neck.

"All right," he said, "so you've only got a hundred thousand in you. Or fifty thousand."

Somehow it was disappointing to hear that aloud. It was one thing to think it; but saying it made the value seem set beyond question.

But that was ridiculous; it only seemed that way. But even seeming, figuring it low was safer. All beyond that, then, was gravy; and barring really bad faulting, it could easily be a whole lot more.

So they could count on fifty or a hundred, and he now considered the spread of that sum for five men. Before, twenty thousand each way hadn't sounded bad, even ten thousand hadn't. And excepting that the vein could hold more, it didn't sound too bad now.

But then a strange thing happened. He began to think of those figures in terms of years. It must have been his standing there in plain sight of the vein that brought it on. Thirty-five years and more had passed in finding it, and he ought to be rewarded well for all that time. It was his life's work, the sum of it, you might say.

Putting twenty thousand against that time, however, didn't seem like any reward. It wouldn't even touch six hundred dollars a year. And spreading out ten thousand was only half of that. Why, it didn't even come to three hundred!

"Goddam!" he said while he figured. Then he bawled it out, "Goddam it, no! Goddam it all to hell! It ain't fair! It ain't fair at all, it's plain cheating!"

He raved and fumed and stamped his feet, and then when words were no longer enough, he seized the pick-ax again and slammed it back and forth against the walls.

"Goddam it, I won't stand for it!" he yelled. "I won't be cheated out of my earnings! It's mine, by God, not theirs! It's me that worked to find it, not them! I don't have to share one bit of it with them! I won't! I won't!"

The narrow chamber filled with his shouts, and the clanging of the pick made the total sound deafening. Particles of stone broke loose beneath the flailing, wild blows and flew off in ricochets that, when hitting him, enraged him still more. A storm of sand and powdery dust, as dense as steam, rose up, choking and blinding him.

It was soon too heavy and thick to stand. Coughing and sneezing, he dropped the pick and backed toward the entrance. The air wheezed in and out of his lungs, and his eyes streamed, as he stepped to the rear with his hands to his face. He was trying to keep the layout in mind, but he went wrong in some way and the floor wasn't under his last step. Yelling, he threw out his arms, but his fingers raked on smooth stone and his body pitched out of the crevice in a wild swing.

At first, falling end for end, he saw a blur of sky and cliff, and far down, a thin strip of water. Then he struck in a slam that plunged him rolling in a tower of sand and dust and cascading rock along the pitch of the slope. The blur of sky and cliff and water went speeding into a spiral from which color and even feeling were squeezed. Last there was a long, tearing slide straight down. This ended in a solid blast of pain, a sense of flight, then sudden, intense cold.

The cold saved his life. He was not in the shallows now, but in a deep pool, and the shock revived some instinct that made his arms strike out to bear him up. By the time the current brought him to the pool's end, he was aware enough to feel the shelf and to know he'd made shore.

He dragged himself up on his elbows and, when his trunk was out of the water, lay flat. He lay so for a long time, only dimly conscious of his face against the stone and of his arms under him and of a dull pain that possessed him. He seemed to have had it a long while, and as he lay there he felt it drain slowly toward his legs.

When he felt this more keenly, he tried to sit up; slowly and with great effort, he got his arms out where he could see his fingers fasten to rock. Still, though he watched them pull, nothing happened. Then he remembered his legs, and told the right one to push. But when it moved, the stroke of pain was so blinding that his mind went dark.

"Jesus!" he said in a gasp.

He was scared now. But the fright cleared his mind, too, and made him want to know what was wrong. It made him remember his left leg, too; that worked better, and he made it over onto his back, and with his elbows, raised himself to his butt.

Now for a time he sat very still with his head in his hands; it ached now, and cuts and bruises could be felt under his fingers. Still, they weren't too bad, though his hands showed some blood on them.

Then, as he began to look about some, the sight of blood in the water about his legs and feet caught his eye. It drifted off for several feet in the current, like a tangle of red underwear. Also, there seemed to be some strange thing sticking through his trouser leg, below the knee. It was yellow and smooth, and the surface glistened.

He stared at it, wondering; then he laughed.

"Goddam!" he said. "I been speared by a stick!"

He laughed again, and reached for it; but something stopped his hand from going all the way down, and he didn't touch it after all. It had just come into his mind that bone, newly broken, or freshly torn from its bed of flesh, was always smooth and yellow.

CHAPTER ELEVEN

Whenever he thought of it later, he'd be surprised that his mind had moved then as it had and that he'd acted as he had. But perhaps it was natural, at that. Even had his head been perfectly clear, even had he not been ordered by instinct, he might have behaved in the same way. Far too much of his life had gone into finding the lode to have it replaced in his concern by a busted leg.

I gotta get out of here, he thought. Then he said it aloud, "I gotta get out of here. Else they'll come looking and find me, sure."

He hadn't worried much about that before, but this made it different. Helpless, he'd be at their mercy; and being helpless made him very doubtful of that mercy. Finding me, he thought, they'll find the lode, too. Then they'll kill me and take the gold.

Then he said *that* aloud. Spoken into the silence of that wild, lonely canyon, it had the authority of proven fact.

There was no room to doubt that it would happen that way. The only hope he had to keep his find, and his life as well, would be to get as far from here as he could. He'd seen too much of mining-camp life to think otherwise.

For several minutes after this fixed itself in his mind, he thought only of movement. Close to panic, he worked himself into the water again. Nearby, on shore, he'd left his bedroll and frying pan and coffeepot, but he didn't bother with them now. Somewhere about, though not now in sight, his horse would be grazing; but he didn't bother with him either. He didn't even think to bind his leg, but only of getting as far from the lode as he could while he was able to move.

For a while he went well enough, hauling himself along, half floating, half dragging, jabbing with his elbows and good leg, and feeling for handholds on rock. The cold of the water had cleared his head so that he knew where he was going, and it even had numbed his leg some.

But not so much that he didn't feel it when he grazed a boulder. In that instant he felt pain that he'd never thought could exist. He yelled—he hardly knew what—and in the black that closed down, he yelled again. In the strange time that followed for a few moments, he was partly unconscious and partly aware of the bottom under him, and of his arms and hands groping for control.

When he came to altogether again, he was partly on a ledge, his legs trailing. Again he lay for a long while, waiting for the agony to change from something fire-bright to something bearable. When it did, he slowly got over on his back and gradually pushed up on his butt and looked around.

Well, he'd made about a hundred yards, from what he could guess; and now, with that much under his belt, the panic was gone. Having got a distance from the lode, he could think about the long haul. He felt safer here, but wouldn't be altogether so until he'd left this canyon. Then, let "them" come.

"All right," he said. "Let's get at it."

His leg would have to come first, for he knew that he could never travel far, even in water, with that bone and raw torn flesh as it was. Hurtful or not, it had to be bound.

His shirt would do for that, and he took it off and tore it into long strips. Matting a few of these into a compress, he laid the others beside him, ready to hand.

The bad part came now. Inside he drew himself up as tight as he could, taking a deep breath and clamping his jaws. Then, while one hand lay on the compress, the other placed a strip for tying.

The feeling was such as might have been made by a blacksmith's iron, a rip saw or the gouging of a dull chisel. He forgot about holding his innards tight, and went loose and mushy. Though soaking wet already, he could feel a rain of sweat burst out on his head and flanks. And it didn't matter that his teeth were clenched: his voice screeched through them in a wild flood of swearing and yips of pain.

When it ended, his lungs were gasping, and his body shuddering beyond immediate control. No matter that he still felt driven by haste, he lacked the strength or will just then to do more than flatten out and close his eyes.

But he didn't lie this time as long as earlier. The sense of having accomplished something had killed the panic altogether, and having done one needful thing told him he could do another, and still another, until he'd made it to the main canyon. Getting that far, it would then be all right to quit, and wait to be found.

"All right, Grandpa," he said aloud, "let's go."

He opened his eyes again, and soon enough pushed himself up. Far upstream now, he saw his horse, nosing around in a clutter of brush, and at first he thought to call it. But on second thought, he changed his mind. He could never ride it now. Slick of gear—and where was that all stacked?—there was no way even for him to drag along behind it. The best he could hope for was having it trail him, and when the right time came, try to shoo it down into camp.

"All right," he said again, and started to ease into the water. He got over on his stomach and aimed downstream. Soon the current bore him ahead and, feeling with his hands along the shelf, he began to move along.

The big thing was to keep on going, to make himself keep moving on until he reached the main canyon. Quitting before then would only invite the others to find the lode, and likely invite his own death.

Keeping that in mind would be his spur and his lash.

CHAPTER TWELVE

Pat McGuire no longer had any doubts that Campbell was up to something. Outside on the oak there was hanging now a yearling doe, a young six-point buck, and the leavings of a quarter from another buck—plenty of meat to last for a while.

Yet Jack still went out hunting every day; moreover, he kept it firmly fixed in his mind to hunt without Pat's company, alone. Coming right down to it, that was the nub of the matter.

"I can't spare no time to pull you out of thickets," he'd say. Or, "I ain't about to waste a day dragging you up no mountain."

Or, "A cripple's too damned noisy in the woods. You'd be worse than on that sheep hunt back in the desert."

It was always one or the other, and it didn't make any difference that Pat limped no more either, excepting a little around Merril and Ross now and then, for show. Jack still kept saying that he wouldn't take no chances on him for another few days, anyhow.

Altogether, this had one meaning for Pat. Jack had come to believe that no gold of any account would be found, and had started looking for a way out of here: a secret way that, when he figured to make his move, would take him far away before McGuire knew what had happened.

Thinking back some, Pat was pleased enough that no gold of any account had been found, and that the prospects didn't augur for more than what the placer put out.

But now he had a new worry: It didn't look like Jack was going to let the lack stop him after all. Could be that he felt the wilderness would give him time to break free. Time would be the same as money here.

All things considered, maybe Pat could only blame himself for what went on. In view of his new ideas on Jack, he might have overdone his hurt ankle. Though it freed him of work, it now had got in the way of watching Jack—just when Jack seemed needing the most watching.

Goddam, he ought to have his butt kicked.

Draining his coffee, Pat took his jacket from a nail and stepped outside, working into it. Now, while he pulled on his hat, he studied the sky. Yesterday had been a fine fall day, the sky blue and reaching; but this morning the air was raw-edged and a drizzle that chilled the skin was leaking from a scud of low cloud that came boiling over the Rim. It went to show how quick the weather could turn here now that winter was coming. A little colder, and that drizzle could be sleet, or even snow.

Game be gone to cover, too, on such a day, he thought; but then that only made his urge to go stronger and his view of Jack darker. He'd be damned if he'd stay in camp with Jack loose in the country alone.

Like a turtle, he pulled down his head, and struck off toward the horses on their picket ropes. Off some, as he walked, he caught sight of Merril and Ross loading a horse with gear for the placer. In his stewing over Jack, he'd forgot that they hadn't left; but maybe it was better that they see him go than come in at noon and find him away.

Then they'd talk—Merril, anyhow—and maybe set Jack thinking.

And anyway, he'd been seen; they were straightening from their lifting and pulling and tying.

"Where you goin', Pat?" Troy called out. In his own way, he could be as bad as Merril. A busybody.

"To catch me a horse," Pat said, "and go huntin'."

Merril glanced at the sky. "Now? Poor doings to my thinking."

"You ain't doing the thinking," Pat told him.

"I thought Jack didn't want you hunting yet," Troy said.

Nor are you doing the thinking, Pat thought, but didn't say. A man could never know. He might need to feed on Matt again, some day.

So he said, "I ain't goin' with him. And anyhow, he ain't my boss. I'll hunt if I please."

"I noticed you left your limp in your blankets," Merril put in.

"You go to hell," Pat said.

"It's funny the work that some folks will go to in order to get out of work," Merril said.

Breaking stride, Pat half thought to settle Merril right then; but he changed his mind and went on to the grass without answering. There, he pulled the pin that held his grullo, led it back to the stack of gear that lay beside the lean-to under the heavy wet tarpaulin, threw it back, and rigged his horse. Troy and Ash were gone now, which was just as well. That they'd seen him was enough; he didn't want them standing around and guessing out loud about his plans.

Not that he was too sure himself. Even on setting out on the trail to the cliffs that Jack had taken earlier, he was uncertain. But he'd have to be careful, whatever he did. Tracking Jack could be dangerous; it wouldn't do for him to learn that he was watched. Could be best, if Pat was right in his guess about Jack's doings, not to stay on top of his trail, but to work beside it long enough to learn his general line of travel and to make a knowing guess at its meaning.

A trail most always showed the intent of its maker; and a man like Jack, with plans to pull out, would hardly look south for a route. The settlements were south. East was doubtful, too, since their hunting had all been west of the canyon. Was Jack to look east, he'd have headed that way to hunt.

It would be north or west then, he thought; and since due north led in time to Navajoland, west might be better. Or something in between that made use of the wilderness of forest and high plains reaching toward the Colorado. Beyond the River, Jack'd be in California.

All guesswork, but something to go on all the same.

The trail was lifting now, getting under the red cliffs, going over the shoulders of rubble broken from the rock. For a while a rash of piñon and cedar grew upon the outwash slope, but soon the ground went more to stone and trees were sparse. Then there was prickly pear and bayonet and, where the stone lay in ledges, sometimes in the warm fall sunlight the whir and dusty writhing of diamondbacks.

The pitch steepened, and he set his horse on the grade toward the Rim where they still hunted these days, since the game was only now beginning to come down into the lowlands.

The benches falling back now; the cliff on his left in massed red stone, light where dry, and rusted dark where rain touched; cliff reaching up so steep that your balance was risked to look up; and beyond, the dim beard of trees that marked the far plateau, the thick press of cloud squeezing fine rain down.

He hung to the inner side of the trail and watched ahead. The first leg went on for three hundred yards or so, until the turn set the cliff on his right. To his left now, and across the canyon mouth, the swollen clouds heaved out across the rolling dead grass and monuments of red-earth country. The creek came from the canyon almost straight down in a lead ribbon passing among knots of evergreens. The sycamore tree, stripped by rain of all remaining leaves, spread out bony arms above the lean-to, and the oak stood near. From the stick and mud chimney, smoke that seeped upward made him wonder if the fire still burned alone, or if Ash and Ross had come back for coffee.

Goddam it, he thought, they likely would. Wait till he'd gone, then sneak back to lie around all day.

For a second, as he watched the smoke lift up and lose itself in the mist and rain, he wished he was there, too; and almost found himself wishing that he'd never set out this morning.

But he'd never learn what Jack was up to if he hadn't.

All the same the notion, once there, stayed in his mind and, as each level of the trail took him higher toward the Rim world of black, dripping forest, and farther from the lean-to world of coffee and yellow warmth, there came even to be a likeness to that time of struggle up the brazed flanks of the Sierra Estrella—a likeness that lay in his mind, waiting to pounce—that old sense of aloneness, that feel of standing apart from the world, and his doubts about Jack that grew bigger in places like this when Jack was somewhere out of sight.

It was bigger now, and it didn't matter that only a sheep had watched him in the desert. Things had changed since that time, and Jack might now easily do what only suspicion had laid to him earlier.

Right now he might be watching from above. Maybe he'd been watching all along, and lay now in wait at a turn, ready with his gun, or to jump out in a yell that would make Pat's horse plunge over the edge. He might even have planned the mystery of his hunting each day; hoping that. Pat could be made to take the bait and follow him.

A sound came from above: rocks falling somewhere. He jerked on the reins, his heart slamming. Jack? Careless with his feet? Or only muddy earth giving way before the weight of stone?

He stared ahead and up, while his eyes went round, the chill grew deeper, the rain wetter. His mouth tasted sour.

But there was no way to tell. He was past the switchbacks now, up in a narrow draw where drizzle and mist were too thick for sight past ten or fifteen yards. And now, too, tatters of cloud sometimes came pressing down to make the gloom deeper.

Maybe Jack was going to trigger a slide down onto him. Here in this high tight draw would be a good place.

He stared, trying to see but not seeing; he listened, but there was nothing to hear now beyond the breathing of his horse and his heart in his ears.

It was rock, he thought. It couldn't be Jack. It was only rock turned loose by the rain.

But I might better walk, he thought, just in case. Should the grullo panic, I'd anyhow have a chance, not trapped aboard him.

He swung down and, looping the reins on his arm, took his carbine from the scabbard. He checked the action and began to move on, the horse at trail and the carbine across his body in both hands.

I'm a town man, he thought in the heave and murk of the draw, moving slowly while his eyes sought sight in blindness and cold lay clammy on his skin. I like it in towns, or in places where there's people, anyway; though I don't much like people. But I like them close by. Not like in this place, where all is empty and wild even in sunlight, and now is spooky and secret and crawling with threat. If ever I leave here alive, I'll never go into such again even if gold is *known* to be in it.

But he knew that wasn't exactly true. Fate, or what he took for fate, had tied him to Jack; and so long as he could, he'd follow him—if only to be on hand to turn him in, if it should come to that pass.

And right now, that's what he felt most like doing.

Maybe fifteen minutes had gone by since the slide, and he now felt a change. Sound no longer seemed to press close, and the smother of cloud seemed lighter, too, as if it had room to spread out in. All at once a break let him see the walls falling back, and ahead, nearer than he'd thought, the fringe of trees that marked the Rim.

He'd come safe through the draw and was now almost on top. It had only been a rockslide, after all.

Five minutes more and the rough and stumble of the trail became spongy forest carpet. Trees stood plainly about, and the cloud was less thick, no longer stuffed into draws and hemmed against cliffs. There was still drizzle and mist, but he could see fifty yards at times.

For a moment he paused at the edge of the dank, dripping forest to rest and let his horse blow. Then he struck off. Tracking on top was different than where the trail defined the way; you had to look sharp. For now, the trail seemed to bear north, running aside the canyon, and inland by sixty or seventy yards; near enough for him to catch a glimpse from time to time of where the trees stopped and space and cloud began. He was walking along still, leading the horse, but after twenty minutes he was used to it and swung up to ride; and while dim from that height, he had the sign well enough in mind by then to follow.

Depending on the purpose, he could read trail well enough.

For what he took for half an hour, it went on north through the steady drizzle, under the branches of pine and fir and hemlock and spruce borne down heavy with rain, and through the mists of meadows.

Then when it veered off northwest, he got down again to study the sign and, to be sure, went afoot for twenty minutes before riding.

Now, too, he started easing off to his right. He was feeling uneasy at how the trail kept leading him deeper into wilderness. By cross-cutting now and then, he could easily pick it up again. Also, he'd been trailing nearly four hours altogether, with more than one up here.

He didn't want to meet Jack on his backtrail.

Still, he went on feeling edgy; and no matter that he'd swung off, the trail still dragged him deeper in. Little sounds began to have dark meanings now: a dead limb falling, a branch swishing up—its fret of needles freed of rain's weight—all seemed made by Jack. Once a water-logged turkey floundered over the trail before him—and he felt as he had when the rocks had slid down.

He was getting in a state, he told himself; and for a time he rode on with his ears set against such sounds. Then, all at once, came one he couldn't ignore; came as he edged by a meadow toward timber on the north. He was nearly in it when the grullo pulled up, ears working.

Now Pat heard it, too, behind him in the meadow, and to the left: a snort. His mind had only one answer—Jack's horse.

He slewed about in his saddle while his skin grained and his breath sucked in. Searching wildly through the dim murk, he swung his carbine any old place at all. Under him, the horse began shaking.

Then he saw what it was: a bear was standing in the meadow by an old pine log. Moving from the north, the air carried notice of their passing out to it. Now it watched and growled, fifty yards away.

"You bastard!" he said, while the fright drained out, and for a space he felt as he had when the sheep had sounded behind him. For a second, too, he nearly laughed. Then he felt mad. Most of his morning had passed in some kind of fright. He had to take it out on something.

"I'll fix you!" he yelled, and raised his carbine a second time.

He fired, and the bear hitched and roared; and *now* it stood up. In the come and go of the mist, it had seemed to be up before, but only *now* did it rise. All along he'd thought it a black bear rooting around for maggots; but no black ever stood so high, nor had a black—mist or no—ever worn that glowing halo of light around it.

It wasn't a black that now fixed him with its mad eyes and bellowed out its hurt and rage. It was a full-grown grizzly, a silvertip.

And now it dropped to all fours and, though limping some, came charging over the meadow like a locomotive.

CHAPTER THIRTEEN

"Oh, my God!" he said in a gust.

He wrenched on the bit to turn from the meadow. He slashed with the reins on the grullo's rump, and drove his heels into its flanks. The grullo put down its head and pitched and bucked.

McGuire swore in a shriek and slammed his carbine at its head. Shaken, it went into the timber in wild panic.

In back of him, the mad, wounded bear came lunging over the meadow and crashing through the wet trees. Its roaring sounded almost at his heels, and he could hear it pounding in the sodden earth and pine needles. On daring a look, he saw it hardly twenty yards behind, and while he watched a lodgepole pine was battered down. In the broad pads of its feet claws ran out four or five inches, and white fangs glared in dark jaws that gaped in bellow on bellow.

He lay against the grullo's neck, so cold and liquid inside that he couldn't sit upright. He pressed his face in the mane, and clutched the neck and flanks with arms and knees, holding on for his life while the vision of those awful claws and teeth gouged at his mind.

Now, for a time, the grullo was his old friend. He stroked its neck with one hand, and begged and pleaded for speed.

Then it was an enemy that schemed to leave him to the mercies of the monster; and he screeched in a froth of obscene words while he flailed the carbine in a wild drumbeat on head, rump and rib-cage.

Again, it was both; so that he spoke in tender and caring words, and in between he drove his heels in and slammed away with the carbine.

Saving flight, his mind squeezed out all else. Jack was gone; had he met him now he would have wondered. The forest was all about, but it meant no more than his reason for being in it. It was simply a place where a nightmare had brought him to be pursued by a raging beast. He couldn't think how long he'd heard the clamor behind, but as flight was now his whole life it seemed a sound he'd heard forever. Nor could he think how long he'd traveled but, like the sound, there seemed no time when he hadn't been driving through forest and mist and dark rain.

But now he made an effort to get hold of himself. The bear was still storming along behind him; but did it seem so close? Somewhere—far back in some other time—he'd heard that, in a short run, a grizzly might catch a horse, but that it tired as the distance grew.

Was the bear behind him falling back now?

He listened for a change of pace, trying to guess. He wanted to look again, but the memory of those teeth and claws forbade it. Yet there seemed to be some kind of change—now that he could think again.

He listened more—while the mass and dark of trees came at him in a rush and fled by. And there *was* a change. The bear was dropping back. He was almost certain. It still pursued him, and its sound was no less full of murder, but it wasn't so close as before.

Still, he couldn't know past all doubt until he looked; and when at last he made himself fight down the image of teeth and claws, and turn his head, he knew it was true. The gap had spread, and was nearly forty yards now. Moreover, the bear was favoring its foreleg more, and was humping along on three legs, altogether.

The sight made him shout and filled him with wild relief. Beside the dark red horrors of dismemberment, there now edged into his mind a hope of freedom and life. Escape, a word of no meaning earlier, now made him hit the grullo in a frenzy of kicks and blows. But even as he heaped abuse past former measure upon it, he felt his throat swell and his eyes smart in what he thought of as love for it.

"Go, horse," he called tenderly—and smashed it with the carbine.

"Good horse, go"—and drove his heels against the torn flanks.

"No lack of hay or grass for you"—and brought the carbine down between its ears.

The grullo kept going, though its barrel heaved and its step sometimes floundered. A soapy froth, streaked with red and watered down by rain, washed over its neck and onto Pat's clothes and boots. But he kept it moving, and the racket of the bear grew less and less, and then was altogether gone. That time, when he looked, the bear was gone, too, given up or hurt and worn down past chasing farther.

Then in ten or fifteen minutes more the grullo could go no farther either; and in spite of all urging and blows, it staggered down to a walk and soon stood still with its legs thrown wide, its head slung down.

For now at least the horse had reached the end of the line. And McGuire had reached it himself, for he stopped his coaxing, swearing, beating and shouting and simply sat in the saddle, hearing, seeing and feeling nothing. Then he thought to dismount, but the memory of escape still lived, and his legs gave way.

"Yellow," he said, as he felt them give. "You could have killed it, if you'd just stood your ground. You're yellow, Pat."

But he didn't care. To keep on living was the thing, at whatever cost.

❊   ❊   ❊

After a while he stood up, swaying and feeling empty and dull, and for a moment could only stand and make sure of that fact.

Then he listened. But there was no kind of sound that a bear might make; only the wheezing of the horse and the rain dripping down.

He looked at the grullo, standing by at a yard or two; its head was higher and its legs gathered closer. But it still wheezed in deep drags of air and eyed him with open fright.

"You oughtn't to feel so," he said. "You'd never have made it alone. I only done the best for us both."

Meaning to be friendly now, he put out his hand toward the muzzle; but the horse tossed up its head in plain terror.

"Goddam you!" Pat yelled and grabbed the reins and swung them back; but the sudden sight of bugged-out eyes and a shaking like palsy stopped him. What was rage turned into something that made him look away from the animal.

Time now in his thoughts made him listen again for the bear, and wonder how long he'd been here. Maybe five minutes, and the bear, if trailing still, might be heard. But only the rain and gasping still sounded, making it certain that the bear had quit.

Unless it trailed him in secret—a possibility that freshened his fright, until it occurred to him that quiet made for slowness, and so the bear couldn't be near.

But it was time to move; and he slid the reins over his arm and took up his carbine. For now, while he felt safe, he'd walk, and save the horse for another bad time.

Likely he was still moving north, he thought, though he hadn't noticed directions in the chase; but the bear had come from the rear, and he'd no doubt kept the heading he'd been on. If he knew where Campbell's trail was, he could tell for sure; but he hadn't the least idea, nor did he mean to look for it again. The main thing now was to bear off northeast and find a fair place on the canyon edge where he could get down. Going back south, he could easily meet the monster.

He went along through the soggy gloom of the forest, his eyes poking out beneath his hat to find the way between the trees and brush thickets, drawing up every so often to rest and listen for the bear. But the quiet behind him held, and the danger grew smaller in his thoughts as he went on farther north.

He didn't see it again as a threat until an hour and more had passed. Then, all at once, he sensed emptiness ahead, and a few steps beyond a stand of pine he came out on the canyon edge.

At least it seemed to be the canyon.

"Goddam!" he said in a shout. "I made it! By God, I'm here!"

At the ragged, stony lip where bramble and cliff-rose—that was deer browse—grew, he looked down; and it was only a little at a time that he began to feel that something wasn't right.

For one thing, he'd struck it head-on rather than at an angle. For another, it was hardly thirty yards across, way too narrow to square with Julius's talk of it. Moreover, the walls rose sheer, with no sign whatever of downslope. And then, to make the wrongness definite, the faint light of the sun at that moment burned down through the gray of cloud and laid the trunks of the trees behind him in bars of faint shadow that met the edge in perfect right angles.

That could only mean one thing. His course had been right, but the canyon's was wrong. Rather than running north and south, as he knew the big one did run, this one ran east and west.

"Goddam!" he said, but differently now. "I struck a side canyon!"

Still, on the chance that he hadn't, he leaned out to look along the crease in both directions, hoping to find a bend that would show the canyon took its proper way, after all. But in the quarter mile, maybe, that this moment of watery sun let him see, the walls went straight.

So it was a side canyon, no doubt about it; and all he could do was turn east here and follow it to the big one.

"All right," he said, "let's go," and he moved along the open ground between the trees and the edge. But he hadn't gone two hundred yards before the bear returned to his mind. Going north, he'd been leaving it, but now going east, he wasn't. He'd still be gaining, but not much; and what if the bear should turn, too?

"Jesus!" he said. "I might even meet him head-on!"

Then he laughed at himself; but he went along faster, too, and no matter that he'd scoffed, the bear remained in his mind.

In fact, it grew larger again, for now the sun in noon warmth began to burn more often through the thinner clouds; and in any part of the forest where it touched, the wild life gone to earth and into the trees with the rain now came out to dry off and resume the day's business. The quiet and dripping forest soon was filled with their rustling, callings, and chirpings. And each sound began to mean bear-sign to Pat.

It was nonsense, he told himself, crazy; but he remained doubtful and fearful all the same. And he kept moving faster, too, until at times his pace became a stumbling halfrun across the rough ground.

Also now, should there be need for more room in which to move, he hung closer to the canyon edge. Guiding on the raw lip kept his eye away from the timber, too—and so would not see bears where bears weren't.

Not that there was much to see below—angles and planes of rock, now and then a runty tree clutching at a crack, the thread of leaden water—but they were things to put his mind on and, in their way, helpful.

And once or twice he *did* see something worth looking at: a beaver pond for one, the brushy humps of their houses, and the small, moving dots that trailed Vee marks in the water.

Another was what might be an elk browsing alone in waterside brush. It was too far down to be sure, however, and in a while it seemed to have a horse look; though what a horse was doing in that lonely place, he couldn't think. Unless it was a wild one. Or an Indian pony.

Just then, as this new thought of Indians about began to grow bigger, he chanced to look east and see a widening in the walls. It was some ways off, but a minute of staring made it certain. Not only that, but it gave out on an emptiness of mist and space; and beyond, almost too dim to see, rose other walls that stood at right angles.

"The big one!" he shouted.

He ran the rest of the way. It would be around five minutes to the edge and now, with real escape in reach, the Indians joined the bear in his mind, and made him run as never before. He ran as if on fire, stumbling and falling at times, but lunging ahead again, holding the horse—which he forgot to mount—until, on bursting through a snarl of manzanita, he stood on the very edge, his chest heaving.

Down below the main canyon reached off, the walls steep but sloping, and threaded with animal trails going down to the creek. On his left he could just make out the point where the box canyon swung past a headland to join in. Opposite the far wall rose, misty and steeped in cloud at times, but leaving no doubt.

He wasted no time on the view; he saw it all in a glance going over the edge, the grullo trailing. The trails were nothing like those lifting up to the Rim from camp; but he could go where an animal could, and he went down the nearest to hand.

Now for a time there was only a jumble of sliding and falling rock, a flying and spatter of wet earth and a tearing through brush patches. There were few trees, and he stayed clear of them as best he could.

At first, he held the carbine in one hand, with the reins in the other; but at a point where the trail fell off in a drop, he sprawled out flat with the horse plunging over him and ahead with its forelegs stiff and rear end tucked low. After that he had only the carbine to keep track of, which was just as well now, for he was on his feet no more than fifty yards in a hundred, and the sliding on his back and belly was all jammed together with his jolt-legged stagger, his stumbling ricochet from outcrops and his rush through seas of thicket which snagged and tore as he passed. Part way down the seat of his jeans went out in a scalding rip, and then he floundered blindly into a ledge that threw him down, half senseless. But it was all too fast and run together for him to separate; all that he was sure of was the fact of slamming motion, of getting down the fastest way he knew, and of getting free of the awful memory of the bear.

It had taken two hours to climb from camp; but only a part of that passed in coming down before he skidded, fell, slid, rolled and rammed to a halt the last time. Under him, his body felt level ground, and he heard the steady sound of flowing water nearby.

He rolled over and slowly sat up. Then he pushed himself to his feet and stood spraddled and shaking while he felt himself over.

Well, the seat of his jeans was gone, and now his bare butt was raw. His shirt was nigh gone, and his chest and back were clawed and bruised beyond count. He'd lost his hat, and the back of his head had a lump as big as an eyeball on it.

But he was whole; there were no broken bones. And he was free.

He looked about while the feeling of freedom at last grew bigger. He'd landed in a fairly open place, some twenty yards from the water. At the edge were stands of alder and willow, and off to the sides deep thickets of brush and ivy that came down from the oak trees farther back. He'd seen such before, but never in so clear a light. The fact of being free made all he saw appear as if seen for the first time.

He was free, he told himself; and then the thought was cut off, and he wasn't free, after all. Hardly thirty yards off, the deep brush swayed, and a large shape moved through it toward him.

It was the bear. He knew as truly and surely as if it stood foaming over him. Though only a dim, careful motion, he knew beyond doubt what made it. No matter his schemes and plans, the bear had smelled them all out and tracked him down.

Though he'd had it only a minute ago, he failed to see his carbine now. He glanced around for the grullo, but it, too, was out of sight. He was caught and chained as if chains in fact did hold him.

Now he felt dead; numb in all parts of him. He'd been gypped and cheated and he stood with his bare butt dripping blood, knowing it was wrong and unfair, but without the means or the will any longer to change it. He'd run out his string, and nothing had made any difference.

"All right," he said. "Here I am. Come and get me."

When he spoke, the shape stopped its secret, prowling advance. It paused, and then came forward into clear ground and halted.

It was Merril's dog.

"Oh, my God!" McGuire said. He could hardly stand for the feeling that flooded through him. Sweat broke out and leaked down, flowing.

Then, all at once, something came loose in his mind. It was too much that a man should die and return to life so many times in one day. It was too much to have hope held up to him, have it smashed to the ground, then have it lifted again. It made him no more than a toy in the hands of a child who couldn't decide what to do with it.

He called to the dog. "Hey, Shep! Come here, Shep!"

At first it held back; then glad to see humankind, maybe even McGuire, it came on the trot with its tongue run out in a smile.

McGuire waited and, holding out his hand, let it down to the ears and neck as the dog came under it. Then he let it farther back and, reaching down, picked up a stone and brained the dog in one blow.

After that he felt better.

That was pretty near all to Pat's day in the wild. Finding his carbine and horse, he headed down the creek toward camp, no longer doubting the way; nor doubting, either, his leaving camp again until time to leave this country altogether. *This* place, he thought! By God, he'd work on Jack to get out of it!

Yet it wasn't quite the end of his day, at that. No more than twenty minutes past the point where he'd come down, he stumbled on Julius at the edge of the water, his beard white on the stone and the rag on his leg red with blood. At first he looked dead, but drawing closer, Pat could see the air suck and pull at his mouth, and knew that he was only unconscious—maybe knocked out by a fall.

Getting down and bending over to look, the horse that he'd seen from the Rim crossed his mind—no doubt the old man had been thrown. Still, he didn't recall seeing a saddle on that horse.

He gnawed on the puzzle for a moment; then the sight of a sack that was strung about Julius's neck put the puzzle out of his mind. From its looks, it held something small and heavy.

CHAPTER FOURTEEN

Troy Ross poked a stick at the fire that had been built outside the lean-to, but when that didn't help he drew the butt of a branch toward him and shoved that into it.

In a moment or two, the flames licked up afresh about the new wood, and he settled back on his tail again. He looked at Campbell.

"You reckon Ash'll try to set it, Jack?"

Campbell didn't answer right away. He sat on a piece of tarp a few feet from Troy. His knees were hauled up into his arms and his head was bent downward.

Maybe his thoughts, too, Troy guessed, now that Julius had been damaged so, and still no gold found.

"You reckon?" he said again; and Campbell looked up.

"Who?" he said. "Merril? Be kinder to shoot the old bastard. Ain't going to make any difference either way, anyway."

Jack looked back at the fire, while Troy wondered if he really meant what he said or was only airing his feelings. Sometimes it was hard to tell about him; but from the little things that now and then let fall between him and Pat in the months that Troy'd known them, or thought he'd known them, Campbell might mean it.

And for all that he admired Jack, the notion made him uneasy. You couldn't shoot a man because his leg was busted, like an animal.

He pushed the new wood farther into the fire, and turned up the collar of his homespun coat. The weather had changed again, the rain and cloud gone, and now at dark a wind, searching and fringed with winter, had sprung up. In the deep, cleared sky, stars shone like awl points.

Even so, it wasn't so bad out here—given the fire was kept up. Better anyhow than in the lean-to, now a sweaty, bloody stink of Old Man Harper's body, a howling cave of his yelling and groaning. It beat all how Ash could stand to fuss and fret around the old man's leg.

Maybe feeling important did it.

In the branch a pocket of pitch flared up and for a moment the crouching dark was shouldered back in the swell of light.

Troy moved his head and looked about. The oak tree, where game still hung, stood clear, and the shapeless pile of rigging seemed a low, red hill. Propped against the lean-to, the pair of alders lashed together as a travois for Julius glowed darkly like two raised fingers.

Just then the tarp that covered the open side of the lean-to moved and Pat stepped out. By his manner and talk since dragging Julius in, he seemed to feel important himself; but maybe not enough to keep him inside the lean-to for long.

"There's a sight," he said, settling on his haunches. "I never seen a man in such a mess before."

"I seen him," Troy said, since Pat made it seem that only he had. Then he said, "Ain't no point in staying to crowd things, though."

"Be crowding it soon enough," Pat said.

"How's that?" Troy asked.

"If the kid sets that leg, it'll need a crowd to hold Julius down,"

"You reckon he will?" Troy said.

"Been talking that way."

Troy turned and, through the space left open by the curled edge of the tarp, caught sight of Ash. Once, two or three years ago, he'd set a calf's leg back home. Then he'd hung it up in a sling in the barn to heal. Now, of course, he felt able to fix Julius. He was dumb enough.

"He's dumb enough to try," he said aloud.

Pat spit in the fire. "Likely it won't make no difference. He could easy kick in either way."

"You figure so?" and now Troy wondered what it would be like with Julius dead. It'd be the end of gold-hunting, sure, if it wasn't already ended.

But he didn't like to think of Julius dead; no more than he liked to think about his leg, all blue and puffed and dripping red. It was why he'd come out here to build a fire and sit. The sight made him sick.

"Uh-huh," Pat was saying. "It wouldn't surprise me, anyhow. I thought he was dead already when I found him. He had hardly a breath in him."

"You told all that once," Jack said, still gazing at the fire.

"The truth, too," Pat said. "I come walking down the mountain and there he was. The biggest mess of broken-up man you ever laid eyes on."

McGuire laughed and hitched about to ease his seat. He surely seemed happy with himself, Troy thought, or happy with something. But it didn't seem decent that he behave so with Julius close to death.

"You're kind of a mess yourself," Jack said, as if Pat had told enough of what he'd seen and done. Looking up now, it was plain on his face, too.

But Pat was feeling too good to notice, and only laughed again. "You try fighting a grizzly to a standstill," he said. "See how you come out. You wouldn't look no better'n me."

Pat had spoken of the bear before. Jack hadn't said much in answer, though; but now it seemed that he wasn't altogether sold.

"Fellow gets dragged through the brambles by a stirrup looks that way, too," he said.

"By God, it was a bear, Jack! Right on top of the Rim!"

"I never seen no grizzly up there," Campbell said. "I'll bet you done as I thought, if I'd took you up. Got snarled up in a thicket."

"Goddam it," Pat half yelled, "it was a grizzly bear!"

"Don't you goddam me!" Campbell came back at him.

"I'm only telling what it was," Pat said, drawing in some, but not so much as other times that Troy recalled when Jack was in a mood. "And I'd of killed it, too, if my horse had kept its head. As it was, I had to fight both. Still I unloaded my magazine before I cleared out."

"And that ain't all," Jack said, "by the look of your jeans."

"Goddam it, it's the truth! I fought a silvertip! After, by the time my horse steadied, I was way north! Pretty soon I hit a deep box canyon and turned east! There was beaver in the box canyon, and I saw"—here he slowed, as if words had outrun thought, but then it caught up and he said—"an elk! Later I struck the main canyon and found Julius!"

Winded now, he stopped for air, glaring; but he wasn't quite through.

"That's every word of what happened, by God! You likely seen that box canyon, too, you spend so much time on top. That ought to convince you; I never seen it with you."

Jack grudged him the box canyon, but wasn't certain about the grizzly.

"Well, whatever happened," he said, "it wouldn't have, if you'd stayed in camp like I told you."

"I got a right to hunt!" Pat said still stirred up, all bristle and frowzy beard.

"Hunt and be damned," Jack said. "But not with me no more."

Here Pat changed, no longer sounding sore; a smile took shape in the spike and curl of his whiskers.

"Ain't none of us be hunting much any more," he said. "Not with Julius laid low, nor with winter so near either. No point in staying on here any longer."

Then, as if the pleasure of that thought had run afoul of one not so pleasant, his face grew dark and pointed again.

"But it's the truth about the bear," he said.

"The truth according to Pat McGuire," and it seemed that Jack could smile, too, after all.

But then when Pat said, "You should know, Jack," Campbell's smile died and for a space he simply watched Pat while the firelight on his forehead and cheekbones made his eyes as deep and black as two caves.

Maybe there was a bear, Troy thought, and maybe not; but it hardly mattered.

What mattered was that somewhere on that wet, dripping day, and in a way no one knew, McGuire had seen or done something that now allowed him to stand up to Jack as Troy had never seen him do before.

CHAPTER FIFTEEN

The fire leaped in the night, and in leaping pushed at the dark; then it would tire and the bed of coals would glow like animal eyes as the flames sank back. Then it would flare up again in dancing yellow and red tongues as the wind came circling and huffing down.

From time to time Troy fed it, then would sit back and, beneath his hat brim, let his glance go back and forth between Campbell and McGuire who sat like two humps in the come and go of the light. They were silent now, but the feeling of the quarrel still hung about like smoke and claimed his thoughts; so that when Ashley came from the lean-to he had the sense of not having seen him in some time.

But he had, of course. It was only a notion brought on by the argument and whatever might lie in back of it.

Ashley went to the creek and in a minute or two appeared again and came to the fire, where he settled down with his dripping hands to the flames.

No one spoke, however, until Pat looked up and said, "What you think, kid? You going to give it a whirl? The leg?"

It was plain that Pat thought himself the one to ask about Julius. Troy would like to have asked himself, but he wouldn't give Ashley the pleasure of knowing he cared one way or the other what he did.

Ashley turned his hands so that the backs would dry. "I'm willin'. I can't say as to outcome, but I'm willin' to try."

"Might put Julius under for good," Pat said, but not sounding against it.

"Could be," Ash agreed. "Could be he'll go under if I don't, too."

"Then what difference does it make?" Campbell put in.

"Maybe none," Ash said, watching his hands. "But it isn't right that we don't try mending him. He deserves better of us than that."

"That's a hot one," Jack said. "What's he done for us?"

"Why, it's only common decency," Ashley said.

"Plenty decent, he's been," Jack came back. "Four months of saddle sores and blisters. A new name for it—decent."

"Well, he tried, anyhow; you got to give him that. And I ain't seen too many blisters on you."

"I done my part, damn it," Jack said, and paused and looked about to go on, but let his glance go back to the fire once more instead, as if it didn't matter enough any more to keep on with it.

"It's only that we got to do something," Ash said, while his hands moved, seeming to grope toward whatever it was. "It's wrong that he lie with that bone sticking out. He could get gangrene, or worse. Anyhow, it ain't right."

That was Ashley's biggest trouble, Troy thought. He couldn't let things be, but always had to agitate over them. Take the placer as a case: it didn't matter that their only hope for real riches lay in finding a lode, still he couldn't let the placer alone. The long ride up here was another: he couldn't let the rain be, or the grass, but had to speak of them in the same breath as home—what they'd mean to those in the Valley.

And what was worse, his way of going on so made you feel lacking and somehow wrong in not behaving or talking or thinking likewise.

Now there was this. He was at them now to go back into that steamy lean-to to pull Old Man Harper's leg.

"What's Julius got to say about it?" he asked Ash. "Was I him, I'd want to be asked."

"God," Ashley said, "he keeps riding off in all directions. He yells about Oroville, then about Marysville, then about how they're not going to take it away, and I don't know what all. He don't make any sense though, that's sure; hasn't made any since Pat brought him in."

"And none before that either," Campbell put in.

"Well, he ought to be asked anyhow," Troy said, "since you're so worried about what's right."

"I already did," Ash said, "and you heard what he says. Don't take my word for it though; go ask him yourself."

But Troy didn't have the least idea of going in there and letting Julius foam and rave at him.

"I don't see no call for that. Working him over is your idea. You're the doctor, or let on you are anyhow."

"I ain't let on nothing of the sort!" Ash said. "I ain't no kind of doctor and you know it!"

"And Julius ain't no calf," Troy said.

"I never said that either!" Ash told him. "But he isn't any other animal either, that you can let the life leak out of, uncaring!"

"I ain't said I didn't care!" Troy shouted, glad, too, now to lift his voice, at least against the sense of being pushed and prodded and told what ought to be done; and glad to see Ashley slip sidewise on his high horse. "But if you cared so much yourself, you might listen to what Pat said! Julius could easy die at your hands!"

"Well, now, I didn't mean to scare him off," Pat said.

But Ash was busy, still with Troy, and paid Pat no heed.

"And he could easy die otherwise, too. Either way, it could come."

"It's like I said before," Jack remarked. "Makes no difference."

McGuire stirred on his haunches, passed wind and settled onto his butt, his legs stretched out to ease his knees.

"Seems we come full circle," he said. "Anyhow, I come in here."

"Maybe," Ashley said, beginning to rise, "but it's the trying that counts. We'd none of us feel right again if we didn't try."

He stood up all the way, and there was quiet for a space while he looked down upon them; and Troy was put in mind of another time when Ash had looked upon them so. Maybe not quite the same, but the end of it was the same, and Troy knew that he was beaten now as surely as when Ash came riding from the wash to face him with his cold glance. That it wasn't cold now but asking, almost begging, for what he said was right, didn't make any difference.

Despite himself, Troy began to get up, and Jack and Pat were rising, too. Then as they stood up all the way, there came from far off in the night the thin, high wailing of a coyote or wolf.

All stopped in whatever way they stood and turned to listen. It came again through the lonely dark, a lost sound, as thin and cold as the air, and Ashley put his head higher.

"Shep, maybe," he said, and stepped away to the edge of the dark.

"I'll bet it ain't," Pat said, and then as Campbell's glance came at him quick and sharp, Troy wondered if he smelled something, or was just primed for more argument.

"How so?" Jack said.

"Just a bet, that's all," Pat said.

From beyond now, Ashley's whistle sounded, shrill and edged and as cold as the air; but when it faded, no answer came. He whistled again, but that, too, was swallowed in the silent black; then he came back.

"I guess it wasn't," he said, but hopeful still he turned again to look off toward the black of cliff and forest and gimlet stars; and in his turning, Troy caught a look of pure pleasure in Pat's face.

But then he could be wrong; and anyhow Ash was making for the lean-to and Julius now.

"I guess we'd best get at it," he said. "If we're going to do it."

⚜   ⚜   ⚜

"Hear the bells!" Old Man Harper shouted. "The bells of Tayopa are sounding as clear as day! Watch for the sun on the mountain to show the way down to the valley!"

"So he's gone down there again," Campbell said.

"Not the first time," Pat said. "Been there two, three, times since I brung him in. He made one trip on the travois, too."

"Hear the dogs, now!" Old Man Harper shouted. "Dogs that bark in the evening in Nacori can be heard from the mines of Tayopa!"

"Been going back and forth between them two, also," Ashley said. "Quite a few times; but then they're only a dog bark apart."

"He ain't really reached Tayopa yet though," Pat said. "Even crazy, he can't get his hands on that loot."

They stood in the heat and stink of the lean-to, looking down at Julius. And he was crazy, all right, Troy told himself; out of his head and raving somewhere down in Old Mexico. Sprawled on his bedroll in the corner, his arms and hands twitched and his head jerked and rolled. His good leg hitched now and then, too, but the other lay still, as if knowing—even if Julius mightn't— that it dasn't move. Ash had cut away the trouser leg and, in the flickery lantern light, Troy could see the bone spike through the torn flesh and the ooze and drip of blood.

"Hear the dogs in Nacori!" Julius yelled. "We're getting there!"

"He just thinks so," Ash said. "But he's gone as far as he can."

"By God, hear them dogs!" Julius shouted, while sweat washed down his face and bare neck and into the top of his underwear. Now running wild with haunts, his glazed eyes passed over them and, when they came to Troy, he felt cold all over.

My God, he thought, it's true! He's all the way out of his head, as far as he can go!

Then he thought: and it could happen to me, too, if we stay here long enough. Then I'd be yelling and going off to far parts of the world. Just to think that he might made him sick and hollow inside.

But it was true, too, what Ashley said. Once among the barking dogs, the trail that Julius followed petered out. Now he lay quiet and sucking air, with only his hands twitching, his eyes closed.

"Can you beat it?" Pat said. "It happens that way every time. He gets so far, and no more. Makes you kind of pity him, don't it?"

"Why?" Jack said. "He's been crazy all along, only now it shows clear. It's all his own way in them dreams, but he still gets nowhere."

"I don't know it's right to speak so," Ashley said quietly.

"You said that before," Jack told him. "What's the good of pretending it ain't so?"

"It ain't fair, is all," Ash said. "He can't defend himself."

"I heard that aplenty, too; but how about defending ourselves? He's had us at his mercy four months now and what's to show for it? Yet we dasn't even hint he's wrong. How noble can you get?"

"It's got nothing to do with that," Ash said, still quiet but reddening some. "It just ain't fair."

"Well, it's so," Jack said. "Anyhow I ain't in this stinking hole to argue." He drew a breath. "Let's get going."

"It's what I asked you in for," Ash said. "Maybe you and Pat'll each take an arm. Troy can take his good leg. All you need do is hold him down when I start pulling on the bad one."

He got down then to one knee. Jack and Pat hunkered down at Julius's shoulders, and Troy stooped to lay hold of the good leg.

"You set?" Ash said.

Troy nodded, and Campbell and Pat made some kind of sound. Troy didn't look, though. His eyes were fixed on the wet spear of bone, waiting to see it go jabbing back into the flesh. Next to him, the tail of one eye saw Ashley brace to pull, and he braced himself.

Then Ash relaxed his grip and leaned over Julius. "Julius!" he said. "You hear me, Julius?"

But Julius didn't hear. The strain of bracing and getting ready had put knots in Troy's shoulders.

Ashley tried again to make Julius hear, but there was no answer then either. Troy began to feel sweat slicking his ribs.

Ashley tried still another time, and when that also failed, Troy turned his head and glared up at him.

"Goddam it, are we going to wait all night?"

"I'm only trying to get through to him first," Ashley said.

"A fine time for it now!"

"You were at me about it before. I only mean to ease your mind."

"I don't want it eased *now!* I want to get it over with!"

"I only wanted to ask," Ash said. "You spoke of his right to know."

"And I'm speaking of mine to get moving now!"

"Hold on then," and Ashley settled again to his grip. Then he looked up once more. "You set?"

"God, yes!" Troy yelled, staring at the ragged, jutting bone.

"Here we go then!" Ashley said. And that time he did: took the ankle and foot in both hands and, like a man who hooks a trout on loose line, struck with all he had, and struck again to take up slack, then kept on hauling while the raw bone went jibbering into the slot of flesh.

A shriek came from Julius, a shriek sounding like sheet metal tearing, and then he set to pitch and sunfish like a bucking horse. Troy was staring pop-eyed at the bone that searched and jabbed its way home; caught up so, he wasn't ready for the shriek or what followed. And when the good leg smashed up, it hooked him in the stomach so hard it left him weak and gasping for air.

His sight dimmed and went double, and the leg slid sidewise, thrashing and pumping. He heard Ashley yelling from a long way away.

"Goddam it, Troy, hold him!"

"I am!" Troy said, or tried to say, but hearing only the shriek that bored and drilled through his head.

"My God, can't you hold him?" Ashley shouted.

Troy's chest dragged for air. The leg was there before him, kicking and squirming. In his sight, his hands had twenty fingers; he reached and grabbed and missed. Now the leg had flopped to one side; he reached again, and missed. And then he saw it under him, and fell on it, fell flat, and bore it down by sheer weight. Then aware that it was solid and unresisting, he lay in that way while he sucked for air and fought to keep the hollow illness in his stomach; only dimly knowing of Ashley still pulling, and of a wetness on his face that was sweat, or maybe blood from his closeness to the soupy, red gap.

Then it seemed to be over; he felt the leg go still, and he knew when Ash drew back and began to bind the splint in place with strips of cloth.

Now he got up slowly to his own knees, still holding to the leg in case of accident, however. Julius lay as still and dead-seeming as his leg felt, but the little air that stirred his beard said he wasn't. He was sure enough out, though; he might have been pole-axed.

Not that Troy cared just then. He'd hardly drawn a decent breath so far, and his stomach was queasy from the blow, and maybe from all else, too. He sat in a dull heap, waiting for things to settle again.

"You reckon it's back together?" he heard McGuire say.

"Felt so," Ash said. "But we won't know till we see how it heals."

"If it does," Campbell said. "He could still cash in."

"He's pretty tough," Ash said. "He could have died right off, with all the thrashing. He pretty near shook altogether loose of Troy."

"Old Troy was flopping like one of Julius's brogans," Pat said.

"He had the slippery end of things, that's sure," Ashley said.

"The bloody end, too, from the look of him," Campbell said.

The talk came and went in Troy's mind, but Jack's words stuck. He touched his face, wet and sticky now from having lain so near the gaping, squirting wound. The warm, salty smell came around into his nose.

All at once his stomach gave up thoughts of settling, and began to churn worse even than when Julius had belted it. The smell and heat and blood and ache of being kicked all were hand in hand against him at the same time.

He began to rise, feeling the weakness in him.

"Where you goin'?" Jack said, and the others turned, looking.

Troy didn't answer. His throat had closed against the pushing of his stomach. On a sudden his taste was green and brassy and his mouth watery. He staggered up and made for the open, half doubled.

"Hey, Troy, what's the matter?"

It was Ash now, or what sounded like him. But Troy kept going, made his way through the tarp somehow, and drawing up outside, pulled down the cold dark into his lungs. But it was now too late for any good to come of fresh air, and he had only time to make a few more steps before his stomach bent him over all the way and roared up in his throat.

That was how Ash found him, doubled up and hardly able to stand. Coming up, he stood to one side out of range and sounded surprised.

"Hey, Troy," he said, "what're you doing, anyway? You sick?"

Troy wished he had a gun in hand; and having it, wished he had the strength to use it. Every bit of this bellow and retching of his stomach was Ash's doing—and yet he had the nerve to ask was he sick?

And even worse to Troy in some way was this show of weakness in Ashley's sight. Three times running, now, Ash had one way or another been behind such weakness. And three times was plenty for any man.

CHAPTER SIXTEEN

The water ouzel stood on the rock. Above it on the bank Campbell watched it dive into the water and walk its shadowy way across the gravel bottom. Here and there it drew up, its head poking, then went on. Now it stopped altogether and, turning about under water, came up onto the rock again and shook its feathers free of wet.

Then, with food in its bill, it went from sight to its nest below the overhang of the bank.

A bird of odd ways, he thought; a gray middling bird unfavored in color yet seeming content with its place in the big plan, and willing to pass its life in walking the bottoms of creeks for food. No doubt he had a mate beneath the overhang—if ouzels kept a mate all year. But he'd have one in spring, along with young, to hunt for. Likely, then, he spent as much time as a fish beneath the water.

Still, it was a simple life. He knew what he had to do. His brain had rigged him to live in ways that would never change. Maybe he fretted over the prowling of skunks and raccoons at nesting time; but he'd never worry about the right or wrong thing to do. A water ouzel would never look back and say, "I wish I hadn't done that." Or ask himself, "What now? What do I do, this or that?" Questions that meant choosing about the big things in life had all been settled ahead of time. He had the answers locked up in his head against need.

Save a heap of worry and wonder to figure life as ouzels do, he thought. I might never have left the Palo Duro, built that way.

Still, I wouldn't want to be one right now, he thought as a gust of wind came shouting from the canyon and poured on past the placer, past the lean-to and down the creek to hone its edge upon him. The damned wind's cold enough without living half in water, too.

He shivered, while the cold wind drilled an ache in his ears. Then his nose began to sting and drip—cold always did that to him, too.

Wiping it on the frayed sleeve of his coat, he raised his ax and moved off to a stand of alders growing beyond the snarl of branches he'd been cutting for firewood. Alders were stingy shelter, however, and the wind was quick to pry and bustle at him there, too.

But there was nothing else to do until the gust blew out, or Pat dragged in more wood for chopping, which would warm him, and he wished now that Pat would get a move on. Drawing his collar up, he poked an eye out toward the crown of piñon on a knoll some way off, where Pat was roping out deadheads.

Or was supposed to be. But he'd been gone a while now since bringing down his last load. Likely he was scrooched down out of the wind with a smoke in his hand.

"Goddam him!" he said. "He'd do it, too, the little bastard!"

Drawing back, shaking with cold, he hunched his shoulders higher. It could easily be that winter was starting now, he thought. Not a wink of sun had shown in five days. Ever since Pat had come in with Julius, the sky had been cast over and snowy looking. The cold settling down that night had stayed on, and each morning since the rocks in the stream were whiskered in frost, like old men needing shaves.

Old men! he thought, and ducked his head to the wind and squinted around at the lean-to, twenty yards upstream. He'd like to see Old Man Harper out in the creek, frosted over; dead and frozen solid.

Not that he mightn't yet, he thought as the tarpaulin flapped at the timbers and a red dust-devil went flustering over the roof. More than once this past week Julius had come near to going under; and at one point a bone-jerking chill had set him teetering on the very edge of the grave. Only Merril's running down from the placer at that moment to wrap him in every blanket in sight, had pulled him back.

And damn him, too, he thought. He ought to leave things be. What if Julius did go out?—he deserved to, having talked them into this mess; and having done so, had gone on to get himself so shattered that they now were stuck, waiting to see if he was going to pull through.

But I won't stay here forever, he thought. Nobody's going to keep me here waiting for him to make up his mind to live or die!

Just then, the dust-devil changed its mind. It had looked to be bound over the creek, but all at once it turned and swooped for the alders. Now it beat about him, sawing and grinding at his face, pushing and shoving him. In one second it sucked the breath from his lungs, then it choked him in a wheeze of grit. Like a boy at play, it snatched his hat and whipped it into a thicket of willow brush. And going after it, he caught a whirl of red sand in his eyes that left him blind and groping, halfway into the thicket on his hands and knees.

"Goddam you!" he yelled as he seized his hat and staggered up; he made for the lean-to now, the alders being useless. Then a fit of coughing wracked him, not letting go until he floundered through the tarp and fell on his bedroll inside, gasping.

It's all a bust, he thought as he grubbed at his eyes, and his nose dripped and ran once more. The point was gone now with Julius laid low—though it'd been small to start with, once he'd seen this country. Ten million acres of sandstone!—and they set down in the midst past three months while Julius fiddled and fooled, went up and down the canyon, full of mysteries and promises and sly looks.

Still there'd been the chance, so long as Julius kept going. And so long as the chance lived, he'd had the pleasure of hunting on the Rim, and now and then bringing back the good day to life. The plans and thoughts he'd had upon that single good day in the Black Hills were still in reach with Julius active.

But not with Julius crippled. The chance for gold, however slight before, was altogether gone.

He blinked his eyes, having rid them of grit, and looked up. In the half-light, he saw the shapeless hill of blankets that had Julius under it. He lay in a corner and, by the sound of him, slept. Campbell stared a moment, wondering, and when the thought came to him, it struck so swift and sudden it scared him.

But only at first. Then it grew attractive. It would be no problem either, he thought as he got to his knees. Merril called Julius tough, but Campbell knew that old men died easy enough sometimes. He had only to pull those blankets off, so it seemed Julius had thrashed free.

He started edging toward him. No one would ever know the difference. Let Merril replace them if he liked; with him returned to the placer, and Pat to the knoll, Campbell could slip into the lean-to again. In what was left of the day, he might strip Julius two or three times.

That should fix him. If his leg wouldn't, exposure would.

Beyond breathing, he gave no sign of life until Campbell gripped the edge of the blankets under Julius's beard. Then his eyes opened. They were clear and seeing, and for a space each stared at the other.

"What you want?" Julius said, his voice thick, but his eyes direct and aware. Campbell froze, too surprised to move or answer.

"What you doin' to me?" Julius said.

Campbell hesitated. It all had happened so quickly—the notion, and the move to put it into action—and now Julius was awake. He stalled for time while he gathered his wits.

"I'm fixing this blanket," he said. "You kicked it off again."

"Y'air?" Julius said.

Campbell fussed with it, keeping his hands near the edge. He noticed that his breathing raced. Julius could be killed yet, but he would take smothering now, or strangling. Still he held himself back, torn between intent and his memory of that good day when decency and the good life had seemed within reach. While they no longer were, the remembrance lived on, but even that would die, he knew now, if he killed Julius.

Then a part of what he thought seemed to touch Julius, for the old man's eyes grew wider and, of a sudden, he tried to rear up.

"Lemme alone!" he half yelled. "Get away from me!"

"Shut up, you old fool," Campbell said, shoving him back. "I'm only fixing these blankets, damn it!"

But Julius didn't want to be fixed. Lunging up again, he seized Campbell's wrists and tried to force them away. Campbell, pushing him down once more, found his hands very near the old man's withery neck. Pure fright came to Julius's eyes as he felt them there and he began to buck harder. Struggling, Campbell now grew excited; then he thought, well, why not? What's there really to lose? He's getting wise; I'd best act before he starts yelling.

But all at once, he knew he'd waited too long. From outside, there came a crash of branches, and then Pat shouting. Without thought, Campbell drew back, while Julius stared as if not really sure what he'd intended, but ready to believe the worst. Drenched in sweat and working for air, Campbell drove through the tarp and saw Pat removing his rope from the snag he'd dragged down to the pile of branches.

He floundered over the ground between them, stooping to pick up his ax on the way.

"Where in hell you been?" he yelled. He was blazing mad now, at everyone and everything.

"Why, up on the knoll," Pat told him, sounding surprised. "Where you been?"

"Tryin' to get warm in the lean-to!" Campbell yelled in the wind. "You been sittin' up there with a smoke, I'll bet!"

"So what if I was?" and what might have been a smile began to work at Pat's mouth. "It blew pretty bad there for a minute or two."

"You think it didn't blow here? I like to froze."

"You look warm to me. I never knew cold bothered you anyhow, Jack."

He picked up the end of the line and now, by God, a smile *was* crawling through his whiskers. For a space Campbell wondered if Pat had planned to let him wait in the cold wind, fighting dust-devils.

"It's more the people who make me wait in it," he said and his hand grew tight on the ax handle; then he thought, shoot, Pat don't have the brains; he could hardly tell the time of day. Still ...

Pat was pleased about it, though; but when he turned and saw Campbell's face, his own grew careful.

"It *is* kind of cold down here," he said. "It must be the creek does it. I guess you're ready to quit, huh?"

Well, that was cute, Jack thought; quick, too. But he wasn't going to be maneuvered, if that's what Pat was up to, and it looked so.

"Not quite," he said, hefting the ax. "I'm good for one more. You get it while I cut this one up."

"Another?" It was plain that Pat hadn't counted on that.

"It could easy start snowing any minute; and I ain't about to chop wood in no blizzard." Campbell sunk the ax in the snag, and heaved it to better balance. "Just don't wait for it to grow this time."

"Why, I never ..." Pat began, but then he didn't say what he never after all. Instead, he mounted and, coiling his rope as he turned, rode off toward the knoll.

A way beyond, though, he glanced around, and Campbell, catching it, thought: speculating, that's what. Then he wondered why, and knew it was wrong to say Pat had no brains. He only looked so. Used to that, you overlooked the chance that he might be using them all along, right under your nose. Which could be dangerous.

Him and his bear, he thought. I never seen no grizzly up there, though once I saw sign. But no living grizzly, and I'd bet that he saw none either. It's only put on to make himself feel big in our sight. Still the bear talk, along with his uppity manner and his queer ways in general these past days, could mean that Pat had something going on.

Even so, he wished he hadn't sent him out again; for now the wind came at him in a blast once more, sawing at him, punching him. His ears began to ache, and his nose stood ready to water again, a bead hanging.

He raised the ax and brought it down, the blade glinting dull in the dull light. He thought about Julius: goddam, he'd muffed that one, and he should never have tried it in the first place. Goddam, but he hated this place. Goddam, he wished that he was long gone out of it, deep in sun country. Goddam, it was a bad day that he dealt with here; saving one, as bad as any he'd ever had.

CHAPTER SEVENTEEN

It was queer how you could slide downhill and not notice it much, Campbell thought. Nor consider it so until you got to sliding in so many ways that you couldn't ignore it any longer. Then you drew up and took stock, maybe surprised that it had happened so easy.

Take this fire, where he now sat in the night for warmth. A week old it was now, though not meant to be. It was really an accident, in fact a notion of Troy's while Julius was having his worst time in the lean-to and everyone shied off of him.

But now it was a permanent thing where they gathered day and night to sit and drink coffee and talk, and even to take their meals; now, too, with the cold deeper each evening, Troy had rigged a tarp across a felled alder to keep the wind off their backsides.

Each of these developments was small in itself; but seen together, big enough to show how far things had gone down.

About all they hadn't done yet was sleep by that fire, but that might come any day. Nobody stayed in the lean-to any longer than needful any more, excepting Merril.

He put down his tin cup and plate and fingered around in his pocket for tobacco and papers. That was something else—that plate, or what had been on it. Deer meat, as a rule, like tonight. Biscuits, too, but lately the flour they'd brought had been thinned out with ground piñon nuts. Not that it tasted too bad. He'd ate worse before and got along well enough, but it showed again how little things got together and pushed you downgrade.

Pretty soon, if things kept on so, they wouldn't be living like humans at all, but animals. Already they lived like Indians.

It was low enough, by God. Too low for a white man to keep his self-respect. Be damned if he'd go lower, or stay long where he was!

Lighting the smoke on a coal, he leaned back and cocked an ear to the wind that soughed in the dark at the end of the tarp. He could feel it, too, some, prying beneath the canvas. It was changed, he thought now, different from the gusty, fluky bully that he'd fought and struggled with in the alders. More a steady, keening drive of cold that from its feel and sound might come from Canada, or even beyond.

A slicing wind, and he could feel it slicing now, sneaking under the tarp and toward the gap between his coat and jeans. Only a touch, but so sudden and sharp that the spasm of chill made him drop the smoke.

"Damn!" he said, and grabbed and missed, then grabbed again. Putting it into his mouth, he reached and jerked his coat down in back.

Sitting catty-cornered, Pat grinned. "Old Jack, he sure ain't no Montana man. I'll bet he's yearning southward now, drought or no."

If only you waited, things came out. It was easy to see what Pat was angling for now. But Campbell didn't care; getting out of here rode in all their minds.

It was plain enough it rode in Troy's. Buttoned up tight, he held his cup in both hands, drawing warmth from the coffee.

"Won't be no closer than yearning for a while," he said. "Be a time yet before Julius can be moved."

"He could still go," Pat said, as if hope for that might yet live.

"Begins to look like he might make it," Troy said. "He's high and low, both, but going up mostly now."

"If we don't mind sitting all winter," Campbell said. "Then in the spring, Julius can come dancing out and bury the rest of us."

"You know anything better?" Troy seemed to ask, but his tone said he knew of something himself, but shied from raising it.

Well, the time would come for that, Campbell thought. The ground might better be readied first, however.

"We could starve," he said. "We got hardly a week of flour left. Come snow, we'll find no more piñon nuts. Coffee's nigh gone, too."

"There's deer," Troy said—a glance passing one to the other.

"Hard to say when winter really strikes. They could easy go east or west, far from here, before they come down. They ain't likely to stand in line out there, waiting their turn to be shot."

"That's so," Troy said. "But there may be other game about."

It wasn't argument, Campbell thought. It was only a noise to make it right with himself that he consider pulling out. Back in the Valley, when the questions came, Troy would have to be able to say that all had been weighed, and that no other answer made sense.

It was important to Campbell, too. He didn't yet know if he'd go all the way back or not. But if he did, it was best his skirts were clean. It was best that Troy appear to lead and him follow.

"Maybe," he said of the other game. "It's a chance, though, if we can't count on deer. Looks like we've outlived our welcome."

"We've stayed past our planned time already," Pat said, catching on maybe, or maybe still pushing his own scheme —the same, if he knew.

"That's so," Troy said, slow now. He looked at his cup. "I guess it would be a chance." Now he looked at the lean-to, where Merril had taken food to Julius. Then he leaned ahead, his voice just heard above the wind.

"You reckon we ought to leave?"

All right, Campbell thought. Now.

"You mean pull out? You mean head south and leave Julius sitting? That's a mighty powerful notion you got there, Troy."

It was plain now that Troy thought so, too; and plain, also, that he was startled to learn that the notion was his.

"Well, now," he said, and hitched and sucked at his cup and twiddled it in his fingers, "well, now, we ain't doing no good here. We got to do something; maybe pull out and go get some food somewhere."

It was a start. It would get him out of camp anyhow, and fix the blame. Time now to make it stick, Campbell thought.

"Sounds fair enough," he said. "We best ask Merril, though; he mightn't like it. Who'll fetch and carry and work the placer?"

It was all the thing needed; the spring took only so much winding.

"To hell with Ashley!" Troy said. "I'm sick of him telling me what to do! I'll leave when I please, and be damned to asking him!"

When he stopped, Troy was shaking, but not from the cold. Next to Campbell, Pat grinned, as sly and knowing as ever, and Campbell thought, to hell with him, too. No harm to remind him where the big brains were.

Campbell leaned forward with his cup. "Troy?" he said.

"What d'you want?" Troy growled. Then his eyes cleared. and his head cleared behind them. He blinked. "Hey?"

"Fill me up, will you, kid? You're nearest the pot."

Oh, Jack Campbell, he asked himself, what's got into you all at once? What's Troy done to you that you should plot against him so?

Nothing, his mind said, nothing, either for or against. He's just a hanger-on, a suck-up, an easy mark. And maybe that's why.

And what about Merril? You're plotting against him, too.

He ain't done nothing either; but still he's different than Troy. They don't come any dumber, yet he's able to stand on his own feet. Still you want him cut down and laid flat; more so than Troy. Why?

Maybe there was no answer to that—not yet anyhow.

All at once Campbell stood up. Driven by the need to move, to exert himself, he headed for the pile of branches.

But Julius had an answer, he thought. Julius deserved the worst that could happen. Julius had promised him gold and, more than that, a doorway—if it could be called that—to something that he'd once had, and had seen again in his mind's eye. Julius had let him look a little through that doorway, then had closed it again. He'd led him on to hope for something good in his life, but had shown him only bad in the end. By God, he wished he'd moved faster in the lean-to. He'd had him.

He came to the pile and began to jerk branches loose from the clutter, heaving them back toward the fire behind him.

Well, he was used to the bad parts. And maybe that made it easy to plan now as he was. When such as he'd hoped for was in view, it was easy to think well of folks, to want to live as they lived, proper and feeling their way toward what they felt to be decent in life.

But when it wasn't, or was taken away, or was held up to sight and then knocked down, why then you didn't think or feel so at all. Then you didn't care about others, but maybe wished to wreck what they had.

He lifted the butt of a branch too heavy to throw and dragged it toward the fire.

Likely it wasn't an all-at-once thing, after all—what had happened and what he now asked himself about. The dark and gloomy side of living was familiar ground to him, he'd spent so much time there. It could be that he'd never really left it, save to stick his nose out a minute.

Having got it bloodied made it easy to return again to where he'd come from, natural. It was good to be back.

When he slammed down the butt on the ground, Merril was there at the fire, filling his cup, and Campbell felt eager and happy to see him settle back with it. It meant he'd stay awhile, and it was his turn now.

It was Troy, though, who started it, maybe from feeling uncertain of wanting to get it started. "You reckon that Julius is higher tonight, Ashley?"

That was like Troy—trying to seem caring now. Well, he was stuck, all the same, and he'd soon be shown how stuck he was.

"Maybe," Merril said. "He's eatin', anyhow."

"Got guts, if he does," Pat said. "Ain't him hunting, or fixing."

Wrinkled up like a prune, Troy's face showed worry and fret for Julius. "You figure he's clear of danger?"

Merril shrugged. "Fever's down. 'Course, it's been down before."

"And gone back up again, too," Pat said.

"True, but his leg ain't leakin' so much. Poulticing seems a help."

"Help more to stick them pear paddles on his butt," Pat said.

"I don't guess he's said where his gear is, has he?" Troy said. "Ain't likely to show by itself, as his horse finally done. Maybe someone ought to go look for it."

"I doubt he knows himself," Merril said. "And if he does, he ain't said. But you go wandering up there, looking, if you like."

"I just wondered," Troy said, "seeing he won't look himself for a time." An eye edged toward Merril. "How soon can he be moved?"

"All depends. Maybe ten days, maybe a month. For what it's worth, he still talks wild as ever. Maybe his wits are addled for all time."

"That was tooken care of long since," Pat said.

"Then there's no sure telling," Troy said. "We could easy rot, waiting to see, I expect."

The concern that Troy'd been so careful to show had come unhooked in some way at the last there, and Merril now looked at him as if his fiddle-fooling had started to mean something.

Well, it was time to end it anyhow; time to stick them both, solid. Campbell took a drink from his cup and set it down.

"Troy here's been saying we maybe ought to pull out," he said. "He says we'll starve or freeze if we don't."

"Well, now," Troy came out in a blat, shifting and scrooching about, "what we mean is that we ain't prepared to winter here. What we been saying, we been saying a good idea might be..."

There he ran out and, with his mouth agape, stared at Merril; but Merril didn't react. He made it appear that he was waiting for more.

Troy pulled off his hat and worried the brim; then, as Merril still watched him in that waiting, silent way, he jammed it back on again.

"What we thought," he said, "is that a party ought to be sent out."

"I guess I ain't surprised," Merril said finally.

"Surprised?" Troy said, as if it was a word cast against him. "How d'you mean that? What's there to be surprised about?"

"Nothing. That's why I said it." And Merril's eyes passed to the others, but Campbell couldn't be sure what he saw there beyond the feeling that it wasn't what he'd thought. It was queer, and wrong, somehow—Merril should be wrought up to have such sprung on him all at once—and not accepting it, and calm, as if he'd looked for it.

Troy was wrought up though, maybe let down now to see that Merril *had* been looking for it, and maybe from him, too.

"Well, my God, you know what's happened to the food!"

"I been eatin' it, ain't I?"

"How long we goin' to last this way? Ain't you thought of that?"

"I thought of it. Maybe not so hard as you though."

"You make it sound like we been scheming or something," Campbell said.

"I ain't said that."

Campbell stubbed out his smoke. He'd like to take things over now, but Troy was caught so well he might better go all the way.

"It's just that Julius is stuck here a time," Troy said. "Meanwhile, the food gets lower each day. Five eats a whole lot faster than two, say. The load would lighten if some was to go and look for more."

Having finally said what he'd meant to, Troy heaved a breath and glanced at Campbell, as if asking, what now?

"Maybe to Prescott," Campbell said. There was no harm in a nudge.

"Sure," Troy said, "we can get food at Whipple, at the commissary."

"I reckon you got it figured put, all right," Merril said.

"We ain't either," Troy said. "We're only talking of it now."

Rising, Merril chose a branch dragged in by Campbell, and shoved it into the fire.

"I expect it's all decided who's going to stay here, too," he said.

It was like a game, Campbell thought, with each knowing how things would go, but pretending they didn't.

"Well, you know how me and Julius get along," he said. "Not that I wouldn't try. But maybe Julius wouldn't."

"I'd hardly be any better," Pat said. "Like Jack here, I'd give her everything. But I doubt Julius would."

Silent, so far, Merril poked the branch with his foot and looked at Troy, who was getting his words together. But then, Merril spoke first.

"And I reckon you're out of it, too. As I recall, you already did give everything; once, anyhow."

"Now I don't like that one damned bit," Troy said.

"I'm only trying to figure where we stand. And anyhow, you did."

Merril put his nose in his cup, and now it seemed to Campbell that he smiled in it. Maybe not, but only seeming so was bad enough, and all wrong. He wanted Merril to be sore and mad and hurt; he wanted him to rave at them for going off and leaving him alone with Julius. But he stood as easy as if they spoke of hunting or the weather.

He felt himself staring at him, as if his eyes had missed something earlier. He saw him as you see a thing so everyday that little changes go unseen. Then, of a sudden, you look hard, and it's different.

That sliding downhill that he'd thought of before was a case.

Now it was the same with Merril standing with his nose in his cup. He was bigger, Campbell thought, seeing his length and breadth and how his shadow reached out. Bigger, at least, than on leaving the Valley; lean still, but filled out through his chest and shoulders where the months of trail and camp and placer work showed most. And bigger, too, in a way that showed in his face and how he stood so quiet and at ease while they let him know how things had been fixed without his knowing. A kid still, but not the same one who'd started out; the youngness in his face was strong and, if not daring, still was asking life to show him what it had for him to see and do.

All at once, he knew the answer to Ashley Merril. He was looking at the flesh and blood boy who'd left the Palo Duro ten years before, wide-eyed and primed for all that came. And as surely as he knew the failure of that boy, he knew that Merril would make the grade.

It was too much to look on him and at the same time know his own chance had come and gone, and never would come again. Every man hates the one who shows him up; just as every man has a breaking point, beyond which nothing much matters. And

Campbell, in a vague way, understood he'd reached that point. Nothing mattered any more.

"You ain't so hot," he heard himself say.

Merril looked up, and the others looked up, too.

"You're right," Merril said slowly, "I ain't. I'm cold."

"I'm speaking of Prescott. You got no business over there anyway."

"Who said I had?"

"You been thinking, I'll bet. You been thinking about the women over there. Not that you'd know what to do with one."

A moment came now when all seemed more quiet, even the wind. Glances asking, what's this? went around, then to Campbell again. There'd been no talk of women before, though there'd been thinking, likely.

"It ain't your business what I know," and Merril stood watchful.

"I'm just thinking out loud," Campbell said, and in a way he felt drunk. "But I can tell by your milk-teeth. Plain as day, they say you never yet saw a woman stripped down for action."

"That don't seem to be your business either," Merril said.

"You're just saying I'm right, is all," Campbell said.

"I'm saying it ain't your never-mind, that's what!"

"Maybe so; but every growing boy should know the details. It's like this"—and then he heard himself go on to tell of Lilly swimming and bathing in the tank.

He hadn't planned it so; all along, he'd only aimed to make Merril feel small and alone before them, to make him pay somehow for what Campbell had only now seen in him. But the talk had gone willy-nilly in that direction, so that the part of him that always did the dark, bad things was likely scheming all along. And not against Merril alone, but himself, too; for in the telling he was casting away his last wishful thought. So long as he kept that memory secret, the hope, however slim it might have been, was there, too. But telling what he'd seen wrecked it altogether.

A man would never blab about a woman he cared for, unless he might be turned down, or beaten out by a better man, and meant to spread his bitterness all about him.

It was queer how he could talk, and at the same time seem to stand aside to listen and watch. He didn't use her name: no need to, for by littles—words and smiles and glances working together—he made Merril understand. With Troy, it didn't matter, and the slackness of his face said he trailed. A man'd never see his sister in that regard anyhow.

But Merril was catching on. His eyes were blank as he looked in his mind at the barn that Campbell built there for him, at the house and its fringe of cooked shakes, and the tank beneath the trees. They were plainly known to him; and when Campbell put a laughing girl in that tank, her smooth, wet skin shining in the slanting sun, Merril knew her, too.

The knowing caught him all at once; he blinked his eyes, and his face choked with blood. His eyes came back from the sight to point at Campbell, then at Troy.

"You hear that, Troy?"

But it was plain they'd heard different. Troy's face was still blank, his mind turned to the unknown woman that frolicked about.

"Huh?"—and maybe he frolicked with her.

But Merril didn't ask again. Dropping his cup, he lunged around the fire. Campbell began to rise, feeling happy and wild.

"You're worse than spoiled meat," Merril said. "You ought to be skinned out and hung in a tree."

"Come and do it," Campbell said.

Merril came, half stumbling, half running, like a wild man turned loose, arms swinging. He came too mad to fight well, and Campbell could have dodged; but he wanted to feel Merril's fists, and when the first wide blow slewed up he stood his ground and took it high on the cheek.

It struck, skidded over bone and glanced off. Campbell felt his brain dance, and his sight blurred and doubled. The bright touch of cold on torn skin told of blood and raw flesh, and the goodness of the feeling sang through him. Laughing, he stood to meet the next one in the same way.

Head down, arms flailing, Merril drove in, unseeing. Campbell slammed his balled fists at his shoulders and head. Merril swung looping sidearm blows going wide around Campbell's middle, mostly. Now Campbell stepped inside to bring them up at Merril's face from below. Merril came closer, and Campbell went back to his head and shoulders. To lengthen his range, Campbell drew back and swung harder and faster.

It was an error, but one he couldn't have known ahead. Merril's swings were so wild by now that they might go anywhere. And so it was an accident that Campbell met one head-on; had he not stepped back, it would have passed his middle, but in moving, he took it under his ribs.

Staggered, he swayed back, sucking for air. His legs turned soft as jelly and his stomach and lungs were unfeeling and numb. Nothing would work as it should, and Merril came bulling in, blindly slugging.

He should have made an end of it long ago, he thought. He ought never have let that first one land at all. He should have been pleased enough to drive Merril into the ground right off, and get it over with. Now he was in trouble through a fool accident, a blind slam that should never have struck.

Still, there was a chance left, a part of him thought while the rest of him, stumbling and dragging wind, sought to save itself in its own way—moving in to clutch and drag at Merril's shoulders and arms and hands. So long as he could still think, he had a chance.

Inside now, wrapping up Merril's arms and hands took all the strength he had, and then he called upon the last that might be left to lift his head over Merril's shoulder. Somehow, he found it, and now he found some to call out with, too.

"Pat!" he called, or thought he did—though he couldn't tell if Pat heard.

But it didn't matter if he didn't. It only mattered that Merril hear, and it was clear now that he had. Campbell felt him loosen, and then gather to jerk away to guard against Pat.

Campbell let him go, and was ready when he swerved. The line of Merril's head was angled toward him just right when Campbell leaned every pound of his weight into a long-arm swing at the point of his jaw.

Merril went down as if hit by a log, flat on his back with his arms and legs spread wide.

But standing over him, looking down, Campbell wondered at the absence in himself of any sense of triumph and victory. All he had in him now was a heaving for air and a dancing of spots before his eyes. In a moment, his wind improved, but the spots grew more dense and he raised his head and looked upward.

Overhead the blackness of the night was streaked with white, slanting motion, and the snow came down upon camp on the wild wind from the north.

CHAPTER EIGHTEEN

The snow fell all night, and all of the next day when Campbell and Troy and Pat pulled out for the Black Hills, and it snowed all of the following night, too.

The snow drove downward from the sky, and came boiling over the Rim in clouds and ragged, white sheets. In no time at all, color was bled from the earth, and after an hour form and shape were smoothed and evened beneath it.

At first it fell in fat, heavy flakes, and settled evenly over the ground. But soon the sky was too crowded for such, and the wind that grew still stronger that first night ground and worried them into grains no bigger than sand grains at daybreak. They filled the air in a mass as thick as steam, and the dim light of the day seemed choked with all of the snow that had ever fallen in all of time.

The wind blew. Far up-canyon, Ashley heard it screaming and howling like a live thing gone mad. It came yelling out of the mouth like that same mad thing burst free of shackles. The trunk of the sycamore tree groaned and creaked, and a branch came down. The tarp that covered the gear was picked up like a leaf and carried off to no one knew where. A storm of soot came down the chimney. The lean-to shuddered and driven snow, as fine as flour, came whistling through the chinks in the logs and hung the room in white haze.

That morning when the others had left, left in the blast of snow and wind as if they'd never get out at all if they didn't leave then, storm or no, Ash went back inside and rolled up in his blankets.

There was wood and meat and water to last most of the day, and no need yet for more. Tomorrow'd be soon enough, or when the blow ended.

Besides, he didn't want to go out yet. Feeling like a dog that's been whipped, he wanted to hide his misery. His ribs and jaw ached from the fight, the inside of his mouth was torn from Campbell's last blow, and his whole body was stiff.

But the misery felt was far worse inside, and not to be seen as a rip or a bulge in the skin. It was too deep for that.

He guessed he should have known that something like this would happen sooner or later. Not that going to Prescott was wrong; it was right that someone go, the best thing in view of being held here and the food giving out. But it was wrong how they'd talked it up amongst themselves while he was stuck with care of Julius and had no say.

It wasn't the staying that mattered. Having more to do with Julius than the others, it was maybe natural that he stay. Its happening behind his back was what mattered.

It was planned, all right. He hadn't been fooled on that point. He knew them well enough after four months and better to have the feel of something stirring. And even if Jack and Pat could fool him, which they hadn't, Troy couldn't. Troy was like a window.

A smash of wind shook the lean-to and a new gust of snow came squirting through the chinks in the north wall. On a sudden, the flames in the hearth were squashed flat by air rumbling in the chimney. The breath of it touched his neck, and he burrowed deeper in his bedroll, while the batter and blast of the gust pressed all around.

Well, he was done with Troy, he thought, and Troy could honey-fuggle up to him all he liked, for all the good it would do. Whether going off was really his notion, or only made to look so, as his manner had made it seem, it was all the same. Letting himself be chivied into speaking out was just as bad as having the thought on his own. Worse, somehow. Likely the idea had been Jack's, or Pat's, and they only made use of Troy's mouth, he was so eager to please them.

Still, there was something queer about that—Jack had never needed anyone to speak for him before. But nothing else made sense.

Campbell. The word stood alone. He could feel his fists pounding Campbell's middle, and feel him weaken and give ground. He'd almost had him down, there, until he'd been tricked into letting up.

He should have looked for something sly with Campbell in sore straits. He should have been expecting it, and known not to fall for it; a man who'd speak so of a woman would do anything.

But he'd been too mad to look ahead; his head boiling so red he could hardly see out of it. He'd been ready to kill in that moment.

It was Lilly, all right, that Jack had spoke of; he'd made it too clear for Ash to miss—the way the buildings stood and how the trees arched over the tank and how she played and swam about in the water.

Goddam him!—that he should see her that way, as no man should see a woman unless married to her! And then tell of it—how flat her stomach was, how she floated on her back with her nipples stuck up, and how the light glanced on her hips when she ran the young bull off.

He punched the bundle of clothes that did for a pillow and looked at Julius buried in blankets in the corner. He'd been dozing when the others left and, by the quiet look of the blankets, still was.

He lay looking at the pile now while his mind went over all that had to be done to keep Julius going from day to day. Soon, now, he'd have to get him onto the thunder bucket. He'd have to boil up pear for poulticing, and how was he to find it now, with all outdoors buried? It wouldn't be far from noon, either, and food to think of.

It all went through his head, clamoring to be done, while the knowing that he'd soon have to leave his blankets made him dig deeper yet.

He hunched them over his head, and for a space lay dark and warm way down. Damn them, he thought. Damn them for leaving him like this!—to find wood, to find pear, to get Julius onto the bucket, to fix food and build fires, and all else that needed doing until they got back.

By God, he hoped they froze! He hoped they got snowed under, or lost—though with the creek to follow south, they could hardly do that. And the country would warm, too, as it lowered to the Verde. Ten miles from here, it could even be raining, though he doubted it.

Still, it served no purpose to wish them ill, since he and Julius would pay along with them if things went wrong.

He punched his pillow again and put his head out into fresh air. Across from him there was movement, and then Julius's beard came poking through his blankets like a badger from its hole. When his eyes appeared, they went blinking around the room until they settled on Ash.

"They surely making a clatter out there, boy," he said.

A week had gone by since his leg had been fixed, but you still couldn't tell from one word to the next what he meant.

"It's the wind," Ash said. "There's a storm blowing out there. Blew all night, and now it's blowing all day."

Julius listened a time. "I took it for them others arguin'." He got himself up a few inches on an elbow. "Where they at, anyhow?"

"Gone hunting." It was close enough to the truth. What Julius didn't know wouldn't harm him; no point in exciting him.

"Damn fools to hunt in a storm, with all the game gone to earth."

"To snow, you mean," Ash said. "We got that, too."

"Snow?" And it was hard to believe that Julius hadn't known of that. It hung in the air like fog. A man would have to be pretty weak in the head not to recognize it.

But Julius had lost interest in the snow. He got himself still higher, and squinted around the lean-to.

"Some hunt," he said, "to call for all their gear. They must figure to camp on the game trails all winter."

Just when you thought he hardly knew night from day, he said something like that. Ash himself had scarce noticed that the others had cleaned out all they owned; but Julius had seen it straight off.

"Well, you never know," Ash said, easing over it. "In a storm like this they could easy get caught out. Wouldn't do not to be ready."

"You reckon they took spades and picks and such along, too?"

"Shoo," Ash said, "they'd only be dead weight."

"Not if they want to go hole-digging. They ought to be ready for that, too. I wouldn't leave camp without a spade."

"Well, they ain't you," Ash said, and now he better put Julius on the bucket, and start boiling pear. Letting him go on so, hit and miss, he might stumble on the true nature of things. He'd find out soon enough, but there was no need to push it.

So he made himself roll out, pulled on his boots and stoked up the fire. He got the thunder bucket in, and while Julius yelled about ice on the rim, got him onto it and held him there until he could balance himself. Then he went to the hearth, and from a tow sack took out a couple of pear paddles and set them cooking in a pan of water.

After all this was done—the bucket emptied and set outside, the pear picked of spines and laid on Julius's leg and removed again, the leg wrapped in splint and bandage once more, there was lunch to make. Altogether this took an hour and better; and by the time that Ashley had washed up, put the food in its sack, brought in some wood, built up the fire again, and got Julius back in his blankets, another hour went.

He was shaking with cold now, and his hands were numb from being in and out of water. It didn't matter how high he built the fire; so much cold leaked in that you were warm on one side only; the other froze, and the only way to get evenly warm was to dig down into his bedroll.

But he hadn't been there five minutes before Julius began to cut up.

Straight away, Ash knew it for the start of one of his spells.

"My God, it's hot!" Julius shouted all at once. "Ain't there no air at all in this country?"

Ash lay shivering in his blankets. He hoped that Julius would let it go with a yell or two, but he knew he wouldn't.

"My God, there ain't a breath in this desert! How'm I going to find it if I can't breathe?"

He was after the Lost Old Woman, out in the blazing land along the Colorado. It always gave him trouble, and he couldn't have picked a worse time than now.

"You stay in them blankets!" Ash called out.

"I'm drowning in the heat!" Julius yelled.

"Don't you dare get out of them blankets!" Ash shouted.

But he might better have warned the wind. Soon he heard the spill and rustle and toss of all that covered Julius, and there was nothing to do but crawl out into the icy air and pull it back together.

"You stay there, now!" he said when it was done.

Julius stayed, but only for a minute or two. No sooner was Ashley settled deep once more, however, than he started shouting.

"The sun's come out again! My God, it won't stay hid a minute!"

Then there was that sound of blankets shifting and tossing again.

A second time Ash got out and made his way across the cold floor in his sock feet and got it all straightened out.

"Now, goddam it, you stay put!" he said.

But Julius was far away, and maybe didn't hear. Ash was just beginning to shake his chill when the sun was frying Julius still again.

This went on for twenty minutes or more, with Ashley out of his bedroll seven times before Julius gave up hunting the Lost Old Woman for that day, and finally lay sleeping.

By then, however, Ash himself was chilled beyond sleep, or even resting in comfort. Though he curled up as tightly as he could, he still shook and trembled, and off and on his teeth set to clicking.

He lay there in a depth of misery, thinking of home, marveling that he ever had complained about summer's heat.

All here had gone wrong, no matter what. Not only had they failed in their purpose, they'd fallen now into spiteful quarrels and fights, too. He'd lost his best friend, and his dog and burro; and all he'd planned and set out to do had gone wrong. He wished to God that he was home again, to see his folks and feel the Valley heat. He'd never mind the look of dead grass or baked earth again.

He wished he might see Lilly, too; and now he knew that he thought of her in a new way. Always she'd been a girl who made him either shy or angry, but not any longer. Jack had shown her to him as a woman; and he could damn him all he liked, still she'd never be a girl to him again.

Seen in that light, maybe what he'd took for Lilly's poking fun at him and making little of him, wasn't what it looked like at all.

Out in the roar of the day, the wind yelled in a blast and a new powder of snow came sifting in. Ash looked to see if Julius was covered.

He was, but he was wakeful, too, again, and his eye fixed on Ashley.

"I been thinking, boy," he said above the slam and bellow of the gale. "What if they don't come back?"

"What?" Ash said, though he knew what Julius meant.

"What if they don't come back?" he said again.

"They will," Ash said. But he still wondered if Julius, in his foggy way, had hit on something. There was no doubt any longer that Campbell and McGuire had let Troy do most of the talking.

Before, that had just puzzled him. But now it struck him as the way they might act if intending to leave for good, and aiming to stick Troy with the blame.

Something else pointed that way, too. Had they really meant to buy food, they'd have taken placer dust to pay for it; but the hearthstone hadn't been touched.

It was colder next morning. At first light, the wind began to taper off, and with full day the snow had ended and the wind had died altogether, excepting lonely puffs that now and then blustered by. Going by the note of quiet and the lack of snow drifting through cracks, you might think the storm over; but on peering out, Ashley saw the sky still swollen with gray cloud. So that a second thought might question that; maybe it just rested, while it gathered strength for more.

No matter how it looked, however, he had to go out today. Wood and water were down, meat would have to be chopped from the quarter, and the stock needed seeing to. He ought to cut more pear, too, if he could find it.

It'd be a whole lot colder than yesterday, he thought. He felt it inside his nose where the thin, touchy skin was as stiff as paper. Under his chin, the blanket had grown out in hoarfrost from his breathing, and his ears picked up the frozen creak and snap of logs. Being out in it for long could be dangerous.

But he couldn't lie there in bed another day.

Finally all that needed doing grew too big in his mind to fool with any longer. Moving quickly, he jerked up out of his blankets and pulled his boots on. Then he jumped up and went stamping around the room in a fog of breath, while his feet worked into the frozen, iron-hard leather.

The morning fire came next: kindling, a knot full of pitch for quick heat, then branches. Set, the flame lifted, starved and wavered into the wood. Fanning it with his hat, his hand began to lose feeling, and deep inside, his bones seemed to ice over. As soon as the kindling caught, he ripped a blanket from his bedroll and, wrapping in it, leaned out over the fire to trap some of the heat.

But it rose up under so slowly and thin in body that it might have spent the main part of itself in getting started and staying alive.

He'd figured on breakfast next, but the bigness of the cold made him uneasy. The wood was nigh gone, and he might use all there was just melting the coffee, now ice in the pot. In the bucket, the remains of the water had frozen, too, and he'd better fill that. Maybe he'd better do all that called for doing ahead of breakfast.

If he'd thought it cold indoors, it was only because he hadn't been out before. In edging past the board-stiff tarp, the air made his lungs catch and squeeze and catch again. It cut down into them like a knife and, when he could breathe again, the draw was shallow. His eyeballs seemed to ice over, and a pain beginning at the edge of his ears drove deep into his head. The whole of his head was growing stiff and tight, as if all in it was freezing.

For a moment he could only stand there trying to get breath and feeling back into him. Snow lay heavy and drifted all about, and a hard, shiny glare that closed his eyes into slits came stabbing from the sky and land, both. Then, on starting for the creek with the bucket, he began to make out the spread of white that lay upon everything. The wind had piled it up into drifts of three or four feet: the saddle and pack gear were out of sight in a hump that came up to his middle; the woodpile was another, also deep in snow, and with branches stuck out at angles like the bones of some great animal that had died in agony.

Nearing the water, he saw its black scar bedded down in white. The shapeless clutter of gray and deep red rock that rose out was snowy on the tops, and flanged in ice on the sides, and all along the course a drift of vapor lifted and moved in the air. On his haunches with the bucket, he saw a skim of ice form on the rim, yet the water seemed warm to the touch.

Then he remembered that the air was so much colder that the water only *seemed* warm; and wary again, he quickly shoved his hand in his coat.

After he put the bucket inside, he went to the woodpile and laid about him with the ax until he'd knocked a dozen branches loose, which he then dragged in and piled near the hearth. By then Julius was waking: snorting, coughing, passing wind and hunching his blankets; but the horses must still be looked at, and Julius could wait.

Up on the bench, where the horses were held on picket, Ash got his first real scare. Plowing up the low grade, a squint now and then showed two standing with their heads down, their tails matted, and their rear ends aimed north, as if ready for the storm to begin again. Drawing closer, he knew them for Julius's, and after a check of the snow packed in their hoofs, struck off toward a knot of juniper where the calico had likely sheltered from the blow.

He was smart in that way; yet on coming among the trees, Ash didn't see him. He walked around each in turn, then he walked around the whole business, hooting and whistling. Then he settled down to cut for sign around all the ground that might be covered by the stretch of the rope.

On the far side of the trees there were tracks, half and better filled with blown snow and, except that he was looking, he might have passed them. But they were tracks, all right, and now and then among them he could see the thin line of the rope and stake dragging.

Beyond that, however, he saw nothing. He stood on the crest of the bench and stared south while his eyes ran and the water froze on his cheeks; but there was no motion, no tell-tale shape or color in sight. The horse could be under any of a thousand folds of land, behind a hundred trees or outcrops. It could be ten miles or a hundred yards off.

"Goddam drifter," he said aloud.

At first he was just angry. He'd lost most everything he owned, and now his horse was gone, too; and he'd be damned if he'd lose that. But it would mean a ragged, rough day of trailing and searching.

"Goddam drifter," he said again, but louder, because all at once he was scared, too.

It had just come to his mind what Julius'd said about the others leaving for good. He could laugh at Julius all he liked, but it had been in his own mind, too.

If it was true, getting that horse back could mean the difference between getting out of here and going under. They couldn't get by with less than two for travel. And while waiting for Julius to mend enough to move, they might need the third to live on.

CHAPTER NINETEEN

Julius lay in bed, listening, his ears tuned up fine to every sound that reached him from outdoors; and when he heard Merril coming back again, he pulled down into his blankets and pretended to be dozing; not sleeping, but not altogether awake either.

Seeing him so, Merril might not like to kill him just yet. Maybe, too, Merril might do some little thing that would show his true plans.

Of course it was a chance, but every day since his ruination had been a chance. It even surprised him some that they'd let him live as long as he had, especially after sending Campbell in that time. Only waking at the crucial moment had saved him then. Or so it seemed.

Just now he wasn't sure what Merril had in mind. At first, when he'd gone out, it seemed he might have followed the others up-canyon. Then when he'd brought in the bucket, and left with the ax, and then come back with wood, questions began to prod Julius.

Maybe Merril's scheming was harder to plumb than he'd figured; it might be darker and more complicated than you'd think a boy of his years would have. Maybe, too, this fooling with water and wood and such was a blind; a stall, while he tried to figure it out himself.

But now that he was coming back this third time, coming fast and direct by the sound, he seemed to have settled on something.

That was when it came to him that Merril might kill him. He didn't doubt they meant to sometime: while he couldn't recall exactly where he'd lost his nugget, they'd likely found it on him, and so it was only time before they found his gear, too, and then the chimney.

They could have already, in fact—Merril's talk about their hunting hadn't fooled him. Even now someone could have ridden down with word of the find, and talked to him somewhere out beyond his own hearing. It could easy happen that way. And Merril's coming back so sure and swift could only mean that all was squared away.

Up to now, and in his most helpless time, he'd played along at being loose-witted, but that mightn't work any more. He might better jump him out, or at least face him. Challenged, he might back off, though did he deal with Campbell and McGuire, it would be different. But he could still handle a boy.

Even so, the nearing of the steps put a fright in him. Lifting to an elbow, he looked about for a weapon, but none was in reach. None was even in sight except Merril's rifle by the hearth, as far out of hand as the rifle and pistol he'd left in the box canyon. There wasn't even a knife or a fork left over from eating the night previous.

Then, all at once, his time for looking was gone. Merril's step reached the tarp, the tarp creaked and dragged open and Merril came stooping in. Julius put his arms above his head, getting ready for whatever, but making it seem that he was just stretching.

But Merril paid him no heed. At the hearth, he lowered down and put his hands and face almost into the fire, holding them so for several minutes before he took a blanket up from his bedroll and, with his belt knife, cut a slit in the middle. Done with that, he took a towel from a nail, tore it in two and put half back. The other he laid with the blanket, then reached for the food sack.

Though planning to wait things out, Julius couldn't bear the sight of such doings in silence. Past doubt he figured in them, anyway. Merril might be making him a shroud.

"What you doin' there?" he said all at once.

Merril turned. "You awake? I thought you was still asleep."

Deer meat, as hard as iron, made an anvil sound in the frying pan.

"I'm plenty awake," Julius said. "I asked, what was you doing?"

Merril moved the pan to a rock near the flames. "Fixing breakfast. What's it look like?"

"I mean about that blanket and towel," Julius said.

"Just makin' a poncho and scarf; the cold out there gets you."

Merril shoved more branches in the fire. Julius rose some to see his movements better.

"You make it sound like you're going out again," Julius said.

"Soon's I get you fixed," Merril said. He set the coffeepot in the fire and rose. "And I aim to be as ready as I can. It's bad enough out there to make a dead man feel cold."

"What's that?" Julius said, on both elbows now; his spine felt prickly.

Merril took his rifle from the corner, opened the breech and began to stuff brass into it. He didn't answer that time.

"Good God, boy, what you going to do now?" Julius said.

"Get a deer," Merril said, "given I see one." Then he stopped and turned, and wariness crossed his face—as if suspecting he'd been seen through. The breech crashed shut, and he took a step toward Julius. "What's got into you?" he said.

"Why, Lord to God, nothing! Why d'you say that?"

He felt his stomach turn soft inside him. The moment to make or break things was nigh, and he could only play along. If he could just bluff through, he might have a chance for the long haul.

"I got no time for nonsense today! I got too much to do!"

"Shoo," Julius said, "I ain't making nonsense; I'm only hungry."

"It's fixing," Merril said, and the rifle settled some. "I'm telling you, though, I won't stand for foolishness. I got a horse to track down today. Cut up all you like when I'm gone, but not now."

Hauling up there, he studied Julius, who could only stare back knowing the littlest push could send it either way. He tried to look hungry.

That did it. The safety clicked on and the rifle bent lower still. Then with a final glance—that might have pretended warning, but that Julius knew for a promise of unfinished business—Merril dropped it on his bedroll and turned to the frying pan.

Safe to this point, Julius lay back a moment, feeling better. Facing up to it was the smart way to do. It always paid to take the lead in such things, especially with someone as young as Merril.

Not that he was wholly in the clear, but he felt better able to handle matters. Now he might try learning the way they moved.

"What horse you speaking of?" he said, up on his elbow again.

"My calico." Merril turned the meat. "He pulled his pin and lit out in the blow, and I mean to find him if I can."

A likely tale, Julius thought, though it could happen. But it fit in too well with his suspicions—a devious string of words meant to quiet his mind.

"Likely went north," Julius said, and wondered if he'd overstepped.

But Merril didn't even turn. He forked the venison onto a plate.

"Of course he didn't. He went with the blow like always. South. Can't you even tell where the wind's coming from?"

"I just figured he might have tagged along with the others or behind them," Julius said, and let that hang.

"What others?" Merril said, cutting the meat in shares.

Was he as dumb as all that? Julius wondered. Or just playing so. He'd best be more careful. Still, there was no harm in a name or two.

"Why, Campbell and them," he said. "They went north, I reckon."

"They did? It was snowing too hard for me to tell." He glanced around, grinning. "For all of me, they could have gone straight up." He set to cutting the meat again. "But a horse won't do that," he said. "A horse'll go with the blow. Mine did anyhow, by his tracks."

Having worked them in, there was more on the point of the others that Julius meant to raise, but Merril now brought him a plate of meat. Guarding for surprise, Julius eyed him all the way back to the fire.

Then he looked and now saw that his meat had all been cut; and that his plate had neither knife nor fork on it.

And he'd asked himself if Merril was dumb.

"You didn't need to cut my meat," he said. "I ain't no baby. I like to cut my own meat. You'd best scoot me a knife."

But Merril just said, "I'm saving time," and began to pour coffee.

"I notice I got no fork, either. You think I'm a pig or something? I like to eat proper."

"Won't hurt to use your fingers," Merril said. "I am. I'm not washing till tonight, and we need something clean. I only got time now to feed you and get you on and off the bucket. Then I'm gone."

Now he brought coffee to Julius, but Julius hardly knew that he took the cup. The full truth had just dawned on him.

So that was it! That was how he meant to do it! Get him onto that thunder bucket—trap him there—then kill him while he sat there, helpless, with all of his defenses down! Why, the boy could give lessons to the devil!

But maybe there was still a chance. What if he refused to get on it? You couldn't make a man get on, if he didn't have to go.

"I don't have to go," he said.

"Don't have to what?" Merril said, gulping coffee.

"Don't have to get on the bucket."

"You better. I may be gone a time, maybe until dark. You ain't in shape to do it alone."

"That's my worry," Julius said. "If I don't got to go, I don't got to go. I ain't getting on no bucket now."

That time, for an answer, Merril stooped and reached out through the flap and brought the bucket into the room.

"You study it," he said. "You might get an inspiration. Time I'm rigged in my blanket, I'll bet you'll be primed and ready."

Panic began to crawl through Julius now. Staring at the bucket, he felt as a man must feel when the gallows are being tested for him. Never before had he faced a mind so scheming as Merril's.

"No!" he shouted. "I won't have nothing to do with it!"

Merril's head came poking up through the slit in the blanket. "How you going to last all day? In cold like this, you'll hardly go an hour. Get up there, now, while I'm still here to help."

"No!" Julius yelled. "A man as don't have to go can't be made to!"

Merril put a belt around himself. "I told you once about nonsense." The towel went over his head. "Get up there now; I'm set to go."

A clock stood in Julius's mind, wiping out the seconds left in his life. It didn't make sense to go on pretending he didn't know.

"No! I know what you're up to! I know all about it! All about you, too! Soon as you're done, you're going after the others!"

"I told you I didn't know where they were! Time you got it straight!"

He finished with the towel, and set his hat down tight on top. But Julius wasn't fooled. They always tried leading you off. Just as they most always turned blustery and noisy when you got them in a corner. Being his last chance, it was best to try keeping him there.

"I got plenty straight!" he said. "Enough to know you're lying! They found it, that's what, and now you're going to join them!"

"Of all the times to raise hell!" Merril said, slamming branches into the fire. "I tell you to behave, now look at you! I try to save some time against a bad day in the open, and what happens?"

The fire built up, he took his rifle and mittens in hand and came to stand above Julius. His face was harder than nails, and rigged as he was he looked wild and dangerous. He still talked so, too.

"You do everything opposite, that's what! Nothing I've asked have you done right! Not once. Now you wind up having a fit over the damned thunder bucket! Why, I ought to…"

But then he didn't say what he ought. All at once, his face softened and changed; and then his voice changed and softened, too.

"All right," he said, leaning close now, as if he spoke to someone far off, "forget the bucket. But remember to stay in them blankets. The fire should hold till noon, but not much beyond."

He stooped and pulled his bedroll near within easy reach.

"I'll get back as quick as I can, but you're on your own until I do. Pile this on you, if it gets too bad. You got that?"

He straightened, and Julius could only nod. He didn't trust himself to speak; he couldn't have kept the triumph from his voice. He'd never before seen anyone lose his nerve in that particular way.

Then, without more to say, Merril pushed out through the tarp, and for a time his footsteps hissed in the snow. But half fearful that he might return, Julius lay still a long while after they were gone.

Then when he was dead sure, his breath gusted out. He stroked his beard with his hand, and broke out laughing.

By God, he'd done it! He'd shamed him out of it altogether! He laughed for fully a minute, until he chanced to see the war-bag that Merril had used as part of his pillow. On the bedroll, it looked innocent enough, but plain as day it said that Merril would be coming back. Had he planned to go for good, he would have taken it. Maybe his shame was only temporary; and he could easy be out there biding his time to come upon Julius by surprise—when he couldn't be talked out of it. A fellow as crafty as him wouldn't quit the first try.

Just thinking, Julius grew fearful again. But his mind went ranging, too, in search of hope, and of a sudden he remembered something that Troy had said on leaving the Valley, about a weapon that Merril had.

A cross-bow, he'd called it, though more likely it was some kind of revolver; and as Merril never wore it, his war-bag might hold it.

Hardly daring to hope, but hoping anyway, he inched out his hand, hooked the bedroll and soon had it near enough to reach the war-bag. The rest was easy. Inside his hand touched cold metal first thing. By the feel he knew it was percussion-fired and, reaching deeper, found the caps and cartridges.

Drawing all out, he straight off hid everything under his blankets. The room was too dim to load well by sight, and he'd best not take chances anyhow. Merril might be back any minute.

But he'd be ready for him when he came; and a good joke on him, too, it would be. It'd still be best to shoot ahead of laughing though.

CHAPTER TWENTY

Mostly, the trail was easy to follow. On the flats and ridges the wind had kept the tracks partly cleared out, and now and then on the scoured spine of a hogback they'd be plain as could be—with the imprint of the snow packed solid on ground swept nearly clean otherwise. Of course it was different in the hollows and on the lee side of ridges, where the trail went under drifts of three or four feet and often took five or ten minutes to find again.

But, in general, it wasn't too hard; and in case of real doubt, there was the constant southerly heading. In time, he'd run it out to the end. All he need do was last until he got there.

He went afoot and rode both, the time to change depending on the pain in his feet. So long as they hurt enough it was safe to ride; but as soon as numbness set in, he'd have to get down and walk until they were painful again.

The horse, a middling gray with more bone than it needed, behaved well enough. It belonged to Julius, though Ash hadn't told him he was going to take it. No telling how Julius might react to that; he might do anything, or try to, he was acting so queerly these past days—way more so than laid to him by Campbell and McGuire.

They should see him now! They should have heard his harangue over the thunder bucket. They wouldn't have lasted a minute in the face of that. And coming right down to it, he'd pretty near run out of patience himself. There at the last, it took all he had of mind and will to remember that Julius was old and tired, and worn down by hurt and bad luck to a point beyond clear thought. Something might have happened if he'd forgot.

At first, the cold didn't bother him too much. Getting used to it was the prime thing: how to take shallow breaths; how to go easy and careful when afoot, breathing through your nose; how to work your jaws so your face wouldn't freeze; how to ration your riding, and save it for those times when you got so weary or mired down that you needed help. And even then, you dasn't ride too long; doing so would make it almost certain that something would freeze. Often enough, from tales he'd heard, a frozen toe or finger would have to be lopped off, and even then you chanced gangrene. And there was no doubt at all of what could happen to you then.

Still, for all of his caution, the cold was bigger than any he'd ever known before. From time to time, at home, it grew cold, and snow would rest on the mountains about the Valley, but it wasn't a patch on this. Feeling cold like this was feeling it everywhere at once, and going numb in one particular place could easily mean that your whole body was in trouble, or might soon be.

There were other ways, too, in which it made itself known —ways that were new and surprising, and spoke of its danger. Once, his towel froze almost solid. Pouring into it, his breath had built up the frost and ice until, on a sudden, it seized and locked his head into it. It took him five minutes to get free and to knock the ice out, and tie the thing back on again.

Another time, on glancing around at the horse, it seemed some taller than before; and when his eye passed down the legs he saw the boot of ice and snow that had built up on each hoof. They were three or four inches high and took twenty minutes with his belt knife to free.

It was the rabbit, however, that fixed the cold in his mind as a thing that nearly passed measure. A long-eared antelope jack, it was the first game he'd seen, and it lay on level ground as hard as a rock. Nearing, he looked for signs of struggle, but saw no marks on either snow or rabbit. Its fur was smooth and unmarked, and the trail coming in from the west bore no prints save its own.

Maybe it was diseased, he thought; but then, its fur looked too good for that. No, the works had frozen; that was what it was. Frozen in mid-air, and the rabbit had stumbled down and died in its tracks.

Going on, the rabbit stayed in his mind. It showed you what could happen out here; it could happen just like snapping your fingers, without warning. It gave him a spooky feeling to think that he might all at once keel over dead, and not know ahead; but the rabbit said he could.

Grown leery now, he felt himself with his hands. He pounded on his toes with his fists and slapped his head until he saw double. Still, while he could feel this well enough, the hurting didn't ease his mind as it had earlier.

You could easy fall down dead anyhow, it seemed.

Aside from that, which he couldn't know of till it happened—if then—the one thing that he knew and recognized was being tired. He must have been trailing several hours, though he couldn't be sure by the sky. But his stomach was empty, and the trail was starting to wind off into a rolling, hilly country below the monuments; and he knew the monuments to end around five miles below camp.

So it could be noon and, from the way his body felt, it could be bedtime. All he'd worn for warmth now worked together with the freezing air in his lungs and the weight of snow in the trail to make it seem he'd traveled twice the true distance. The snow and ice that grew at all times on his boot-soles seemed to grow thicker, and faster, too. The towel bowed his head, freighted in ice. The blanket pressed on his shoulders, and snow fringing the bottom of it dragged from below.

Ever since finding the rabbit he'd been careful of riding much, and that didn't help things. Nor did leaving camp without food to nibble on during the day.

Maybe in such weather a man could starve to death, as well as freeze, and not know what was wrong. He surely could get weary and weak—that he knew—and yet not feel too hungry. Unless the cold and weariness bore too heavily on him to let him feel hungry.

He thought of the rabbit again; maybe the rabbit had starved, though it hadn't looked so. Hunger traveled with wild things, however.

But that was beside the point. The main thing now was getting back while he had strength to make it in good order. He could maybe trail another hour, but he could easily overreach himself, too. Going downgrade was different than climbing, as returning would call for. Dark could catch him, too, if he dragged it out too long; and then perhaps the dead, dead cold of dark. Then there was Julius to think of, lying alone and sick and full of wild notions. It was hard to see how he could last long alone; a fit might even send him crawling outdoors.

Still, it graveled him to quit a trail so plain to see. He might come up with the calico any minute now, holed up in a draw, or behind an outcrop. Having lost so much already made it hard to quit on a chance that might be near.

He came to a point where the ground went into an arroyo, and there drew up to look about, while the two ideas pulled at him. If he headed back now, he'd make camp in good light; while going on another hour could make getting back chancy.

His eye, while he backed and filled in his mind, passed down the long arm of the draw. Had he been a bird that saw it in flight, it might have seemed a hand and fingers reaching out from a wrist. Where he stood would be the forearm. The calico's tracks were in plain sight.

Well, why not? It wouldn't take long to scout it out; not an hour, anyhow. Moreover, it looked to be a place where a horse might lie up a while—deep and brushy, with walls and outcrops as windbreaks.

It was a good enough compromise, and he descended on the trail, plainer now than ever here because the snow had settled down beneath the overhang of the walls, and the backwind had stacked it into drifts. He went along, the pitch growing steeper, and the snow, as the trail came more and more beneath the overhang, deeper about him. Had he not been on a broken trail, he'd never have dared set foot in such country in this weather; but with even the worst smashed down ahead of him, the growing depth was harder to manage than he'd thought it would be.

Now for a space he rested, watching the black worms squirming in his sight, while the cold air plunged in. Beyond him, as his eyes cleared, the arm began to let down toward the hand, it looked like. But between, at what would be the wrist, the walls pressed in close, and here the snow was piled deeper than any he'd seen so far. Yet the calico had made his way through, and had spread a wide trail, too.

"Where he went, I can go," he said. But I'd best ride, he thought, and he gathered the reins and raised up into the icy saddle.

At first all went well. Then as he drew nearer, a widening in the trail developed as a place where the calico had cast about to get through, chopping this way and that with its hoofs and legs as it floundered around. At one point, it looked to have gone down.

The sight made him wary of bulling through on the horse, and he got down again. The reins on his arm, he stepped ahead to the edge. Here, even in broken ground, the snow reached his knees, and the following step, one that was an error as he leaned to look, bore him down to his waist.

"Ho!" he shouted, and swung his arms to regain balance. Behind the horse reared in fright, and dragged him altogether off his feet; now he plunged headlong into unbroken snow, stretched out to full length by the reins still looped on his arm.

All around snow pressed down, casing him in. Daylight filtered in from above, a grayness in his eyes, and floods of snow drove down his neck and up his wrists. For one blind second, panic seized him, and he jerked and bucked and threshed until his head broke clear.

Now he lay quiet a time, looking. He was off the trail by three or four feet in snow up to his neck. His feet and legs had gone down almost straight in his panic, and now he felt them tangled in brush unseen from above. It was easy to tell why the calico'd floundered.

"Damn fool!" he said, while his breath wracked him and the light went dim and bright and dim and bright. "No brains at all."

Disgust made him angry; the anger made him struggle still more, and the struggle drove him deeper. Then the flat sounding hammer of his heart high up in his head made him stop.

"All right, think!" he said.

He thought, and sent his free hand down his legs. It touched the clutching branches but, through the heavy wool mitten, learned nothing. Then, as of its own mind, the mitten slipped off, and he felt the smooth rounded shapes that held him fast. But so quickly did the cold numb his fingers that feeling was gone before he could spring the trap.

Well, he still had his knife, and now he knew the knife would be his only chance to get out in one piece; the horse could back him out, no doubt, but that would mean a broken leg, and if he scared it, he might lose his grip on the reins and never get out.

So the knife had to do it. He jerked it from his belt, clamping the handle in his numbing hand as best he could, and holding firm to the reins with the other. Then, careful not to scare the horse, he bulled around with his shoulders until the roots were open to light; then plunged down the blade as a wedge between the frozen branches.

Now he leaned on it; a little give told him he was making headway. He leaned harder, with all of his strength and weight; and he could feel the pressure leave his foot. Once more, and calling now on all the strength and power that he had left in him, calling up to the limit and past the limit, until sight became a red haze, he bore upon the heavy blade; until in one instant, when time and strength of steel and ridged muscle and shaped root and bonded ice stood still in equal balance—the last extreme of power prevailed and, sounding like a rifle in the confines of the hole, the bright steel snapped, the root-wood splintered into fragments and the bond of ice shattered like glass.

But he was free. His foot came up as if never held. In one motion, taking no chance on being caught again, he flung himself up and out and, falling, lay in the snow as a swimmer, above the branches' grasp.

Now he called to the horse, telling it to back. Standing over him a few feet off on fair ground, its face was masked in frost, and a rime of ice strung from its muzzle. Not understanding at first, it simply stared down at him in dumb misery.

"Back!" he called again. "Back, now!"—but quietly, to make it seem that there was nothing strange in how he lay, that he did so often when the mood struck him. "Back now, back up, horse."

Then it seemed to have a glimmer of understanding, after all. And if doubtful of his behavior, still its wariness was dulled by his voice and slowly it started backing. A little at a time it drew him out and, on feeling it pulling well, he threw his legs and arms in motion to help, and plowed and drove on to solid ground.

With what he had left, he got to his knees and, brain hung dark with gray curtains, felt his way to a foreleg and as he would with a tree, dragged up hand over hand to his feet. And so that he wouldn't quit now, reached and grasped the mane and kept on dragging and hauling until he was astride; then, with the reins looped over the head, in some way made a final drive to square himself and turn the horse on the backtrail.

The last clear thing that he remembered as a conscious effort for some time after was to put his bare hand inside the blanket he wore.

❧ ❧ ❧

The rest of that day came to him in patches, some fairly clear and others gray and dark with only a dim notion of being and movement.

Time had no measure any longer: the horse went out of the draw and struck off north upon the old trail. But he knew it only as the grade changed; he didn't wonder when he got there, or even how long before he knew he had. It could be an hour, or any small part of it; it could be more, too, but to bother his head with it was too much. The thought would come to the edge of his mind, look in, then go away.

It was the same with other parts of the land; what he'd taken care to note earlier, now meant nothing. In one moment of clear sight and mind, he saw the reach and color of the monuments ahead—and in that moment thought, I'm still south of them. But in another, when he found himself well into them, he had no idea when either time came about, or even which came first.

Time before had been measured by how long he could ride before the numbing of his feet told him to walk; and guessed at again by how long he walked before the pain was sharp enough to let him ride again. These, taken together, along with his knowing the country's features, had given a fair count of the hours.

But that was all changed now. Riding, his fight and struggle had gone, and he lay on the point of sleep. At no other time could he remember such total weariness. Like a river it drained each part of him, dark edged at his mind, and worked toward his eyes. The cold no longer pinched and gnawed; his body seemed closed in warm comfort.

It was that which finally made him aware of his condition. The warmth scared him; warmth and drowsiness in the midst of great cold could take him off into death.

All at once he felt himself swaying, woke enough to see the white world turning and, on the point of falling, reached to save himself.

He sat up straight and for a time beat himself about the body with his arms. Then, breathless, he recalled the rope and, working it free of the thong, drew the loop over his middle and bound the fall of the rope around himself and around the cantle and horn of the saddle.

But that only kept him on the horse, or partly on. It didn't keep him awake, and it was the raw jerk of the rope that brought him to next time, as he dangled halfway down to the ground.

So now he had to walk a while, or else go sleeping into death, unknowing. With the end of the rope made fast to the horn, he paid out the rest and, rolling and sliding, let himself down.

Landing, he felt the jar, but in stepping out, he sprawled. Working to his knees, he got to his feet, and fell again. Now he lay for a time, warm and at ease in the soft snow, uncaring.

I don't want to get up, he thought; don't want to go no farther. Too much work, and nothing works, anyhow. Just want to lie here where it's warm and pleasant.

He hadn't felt so comfortable in a long while, maybe since leaving home; and now the feeling made home big in his mind. The words in his thoughts took on the sound of other voices.

Pa was talking, all at once, telling of the Valley's plight.

"Got to hold on," he seemed to say. "Got to hold on and keep on going till it betters. Ain't nothing else to do."

He almost laughed, hearing that. It was why he'd left, and here he was in this fix.

The words stuck, though, stuck and went on again and again.

"Keep going," they seemed to say. "Got to hold on and keep going."

Then he was back in the snow on his belly, and the words were his.

"Got to keep going," his voice said. "Keep going and hold on."

So he tried again to get up; then he thought to heave a chunk of snow at the rump of the horse, and yell, "G'wan, get moving!" And, maybe no longer surprised at his ways, the horse went on.

It drew him erect, and with his weight against the pull he was able to take a few steps before he went wrong and sprawled again.

But the horse kept moving along now, and soon enough he tried again; and while he fell then, too, he kept on working at it, and by and by he had feeling in his legs, and in good time was afoot more than down.

Sometimes, after a while, he rode again, whoaing the horse and scrabbling up into the saddle; but as the voice in his mind kept telling him to hold on, to keep on going, he was fearful of rest and would soon drop down once more to stagger and sprawl and get up and go on at the end of the line.

Time was strange as ever all this while, with only motion and dim land shapes to mark that it existed at all. And so he was surprised, in one particular moment, to see ahead what seemed a building.

Then he knew it for one; it was the lean-to standing in the late gray of the day, heaped in snow, but with timber ends in plain sight.

A sound left his throat. He dropped the line, stumbled a few steps and went flat. Getting up, he struck out again, plunging and weaving; falling that time, he struck in a roll and, sitting up, pulled off his boots and socks and threw them toward the tarp at the opening.

He covered what was left on his hands and knees, lunging past the tarp. Inside it was close to pitch-dark, but there was still in the hearth a spark of the day's burning. The sight made him shiver and begin to shake all over, for you were never so cold as when the prospect of warmth was near.

"Merril?" It was Julius calling now from his corner.

Ashley turned toward the sound, seeing only a line that seemed to glint in the dark. But he smelled him. He crawled toward his bedroll.

"You done it, all right, I reckon," he said. "Just as I thought."

"I see you sneaking up!" Julius shouted. "Keep clear of me!"

"I ain't going to touch you. You can sleep in it."

"I'll fix you!" Julius yelled.

The line that Ash had seen moved now to follow him. Of a sudden, he knew what it was, and made a dive and reach, and when his hand closed over the barrel he jerked it free. Julius howled, and Ashley swung his arm back, aiming at his head.

"I'm gonna knock your brains out!" he said.

Then in mid-air his hand slowed, slowed more and stopped; even in his misery of cold and feeling stranded in a land of winter he felt shamed. A man so crazy as to shoot over getting onto a thunder bucket had no brains; not any longer, anyhow. It was plainer now than it ever had been before.

"No, I ain't either," he said and brought the gun down all the way. He could tell by the feel it was his, and he slipped it into his war-bag. "But you can sleep in your damned mess, all the same."

Julius made some kind of raving, strung-out noise, but Ash paid him no more heed. Pulling his blankets toward the hearth, he shoved the few branches left into the fire, then crawled down deep in his bedroll, curling up in a ball and rubbing his bare feet with his hands.

Imagine a thing like that, he thought as the shakes of growing warmth took hold. A good thing Julius hadn't known about the sear in that pistol; that it couldn't be fired except by loosing the hammer. He'd have to be careful around him now.

Outside, in the creep and steal of the winter evening, the wind began to grow again, and there came the sound of new blown snow against the tarp, hard and grainy to the ear, the coldest snow of all.

Hold on, he thought, hearing it. Hold on and keep on going is all there is until things better; and you got to believe that they will.

CHAPTER TWENTY-ONE

"What about that pine thicket up there?" Troy turned and asked. "You reckon that's all right for camp? It's coming on dark soon."

McGuire put his head up and looked beyond Troy, who now rode in front, breaking trail up the side of the Black Hills. The pine that he spoke of lay in a saddle, a kind of sag in the ridgepole of the mountain. It looked thick enough, and there seemed to be no other stand of trees that might be nearer.

"It looks all right from here. Might as well point for it."

"You want to ask Jack?" Troy said, as if it must be cleared with Campbell first.

But McGuire wasn't going to ask Jack anything. "What for? Nothing's closer. Go ahead and point for it."

For a second doubt showed in Troy's face; but then he heaved his shoulders and faced around front again. Pat watched him for a space, then glanced to his rear, wondering if Jack heard; not that he cared. But it was sure that he hadn't, for only now was he coming out of a draw below them, the pack string in tow. For another space he watched him, too, half wishing that he had heard, and then his eye was drawn by what lay beyond.

They were high on the side of the Hills now, and he could look down and see the Verde in a dull trickle of metal, like lead spilled from a bullet mold. Beyond, the snowy valley rolled northward up the benches into rimrock; and beyond that the white land just went on and on until it lost itself against the cliff and canyon country that they'd left yesterday. In the failing light of the day, the broken face of the Rim no longer had any color and, at that distance, not much shape either.

He turned about, a shiver jarring him. He'd never been so cold in his life as on coming down through the roar and ice of the blizzard, feeling their way along the creek until, on a sudden, they'd felt the warm breath of the Verde in their faces. Maybe not warm exactly, but not so freezing as before.

It was queer how that could happen in a bare twenty or twenty-five miles. The change in height, no doubt; they must have let down a thousand or two feet. Then, too, the river'd be warmer than the air. Even up here on the mountain, it was warmer, he thought as he glanced ahead and upward toward the pine where, in half an hour maybe, they'd make camp; the air of the Verde still held, lifting up.

And once across the ridgepole, the harder weathers of the north might be left behind altogether.

So he guessed he ought to be pleased, pleased at least to be shed of that wilderness land with its dim lift of forest and cliff, its awful bears and its cold so sudden and hard.

But he didn't feel so. Or anyhow his pleasure wasn't what it should be. He was glad enough to be warm again, but there it ended. Something else, a sense of having won out, that he also should have felt, was missing.

It was Jack, that's what it was. It was damned old Jack and how he'd set things up and got them moving from camp. All along there for ten days or so, he'd been working on Jack's mind toward that same end; but it hadn't turned out as he'd figured. In the crucial moment, Jack had taken the play from his hands altogether.

With two days now to think of it on the trail, he'd come to see it as wrong, too, and not at all as he'd planned it.

They were leaving, all right, but not as he'd figured. He'd wanted Jack to cave in and quit outright. He'd wanted him to be so worn down by thoughts of no gold, of bad weather, of four months of hopeless, pointless work and effort, that he would, in so many words, throw down the tools and say, "To hell with it! Let's go!"

But he hadn't done anything like that. Instead he'd told a tale that made Pat's hair stand on end, and then he'd knocked young Merril into a cocked hat. And on the point of leaving, he'd rigged it up to pin the whole business on Troy.

Which only went to show again that you could never tell exactly what was going on in Jack's thoughts.

Not that Pat felt any better for being reminded on that point. He felt cheated all the same, and it was firmly fixed in his head that, in some way or other, Jack should pay for that. He should be made to know that he wasn't as hot as he no doubt thought he was.

There was plenty he didn't know; and Pat wished he knew a way to let Jack wonder what, and still keep it secret. That'd cool him off.

The way broadened and grew level for a time, and Jack drew nearer with the pack string. Then at the point where it steepened again, Pat stood down to clean the hoofs of his horse, to ease the new climb.

It was there that Jack came up behind him and drew to a halt, waiting. For a while, he sat silent, watching. Then he said, "You could lay an egg and hatch it in the time you're taking to do that. Even in the snow, you could."

Pat was getting on as best he could but, on hearing that, he took his time. He wouldn't be pushed around by Jack any longer.

"I guess you want the trail broke, don't you?"

"You could easy move over and let me by," Jack said. "It's wide enough. Passing later would be no chore. For them that know how."

In his hand, Pat's knife moved still slower. He picked at a piece of ice with his fingernail.

"Moving over might end me up on the river bank," he said.

"Letting a pack string take root in such a place ain't the peak of wisdom either. They start looking around and thinking where they are."

"A breather won't hurt 'em none."

"Maybe you'll take 'em on then, since you're all at once so full of feeling for them."

"It ain't my turn," Pat said. "I already drug 'em halfway up. Don't let that slip your mind. We all got to do our share of the work."

"Ha! You sermonizing on work."

Pat stalled as long as he could. Then when there was no more ice to dig, he put the knife in his belt and got back into the saddle. Lining out on the grade, he glanced around at Jack and the string behind. The horses had their heads down, and were plodding up in good order. There wasn't any reason not to call that fact to Jack's notice.

"Don't look to me like that halt did any harm," he said. "They're coming along as good as ever; better, maybe."

But Jack wasn't dwelling on it any longer. He didn't even look when Pat spoke; his eye had gone past and now was on Troy, a few hundred yards beyond them up the slope.

"Where's he making for?" he said in a moment. "Or does he know?"

"That saddle yonder," Pat told him. "We figured on making camp there tonight."

"Oh, did we?" Jack said. "I hadn't heard before."

A choice had come to Pat. He could leave it be, or take it up; and if Jack's tone had been different, he'd have left it. But the sound had a note of challenge and asked for an answer.

"I don't see none better right off, do you?"

"Be better on the yon side of it," Jack said.

"How do you figure that?" Pat said, turning to look at him. "You don't know what's over there. You can't see it."

"Don't have to. I'm going by how the weather comes. Been blowing from the north, so we'd need your saddle behind us to be out of it."

A detail, it was; a little nit-picking detail. Once among the trees, they could easy cross the ridge, and if need be, drop down a way. It was something to be done without thought, a matter of course. But Jack made it sound as if it never *would* be done; even if the wind nigh knocked them off their feet. And it wasn't even blowing. But since Jack chose to split hairs, he might as well have that pointed out to him, too.

"Not yet, no," Jack said in answer. "But it could start again soon enough. You ever camp in a saddle during a blow? A good one'll skin you out."

"Why go begging trouble?" Pat said.

"I ain't. I'm just scouting it."

"Well, the wind ain't blowing yet," Pat told him again.

"Be smart to plan on it though," Jack came back. "Be smart, too, to plan on moving over below that saddle. When we get up here a ways, I'll just wave Troy on."

McGuire didn't say anything to that remark. He couldn't trust himself to speak out one way or the other. Something like a big, round bubble, made of all Jack's slights, his lording-over-you ways, his sly tricks and know-it-all, was swelling black in his mind.

He rode along up the grade for a hundred yards or better in silence, waiting for it to leave or grow smaller. But it wouldn't do either. Instead, it grew fatter and more shiny, until it was so swollen with past remembrances of Jack's belittling and meanness that he felt it would burst—and no matter the danger that could mean.

But it was Jack who spoke first again—still on the state of the weather. It was never enough that he only catch you out on a point. Once started, he wouldn't let go until you looked like a fool.

"Hey, Pat," he called out all at once. "Put your face up."

Without thought, Pat did so; then it flashed in his mind that, unasking, he had bent again to Jack's bidding—and he jerked his head down again. But not before he'd felt the sting of fine grains, as hard and small as table salt, on his cheek.

"That was snow you took a sniff of there," Jack called out. "Take another, you might smell a breeze pushing." He laughed, and now the air *did* move, and brought the laugh pressing all about Pat. "Go on, Pat, don't let pride get in your way."

In Pat's head the bubble swelled, and swelled again. There seemed no room for anything except pure hate. All else was pushed aside, or squeezed into far corners.

"You go to hell!" he turned and yelled. "You know so damned much!"

Jack laughed again. "I know what the weather's doing. A man'd be a pure fool not to know; or not to admit it when he does know."

The bubble in Pat's head broke. Like a boil that bursts and squirts out its fester of pus, the black and glistening poison held in Pat's mind seeped down through all of him. It filled his ears with the sound of roaring, and all in his sight went dark. His mouth tasted rusty.

"And that's about the size of what you *do* know!" he heard himself shout. "But it don't come even knee-high to what I know!"

"If you're speaking of me, you'd damned well better be careful," Jack called, still in a laughing mood, but looking to change.

"It's a whole lot bigger than your pint-sized doings!" Pat shouted back. "What I know makes our pulling out of this country the biggest joke in the world!"

The little that was left of Pat's sense said it was an error for him to say that. But he was past listening to sense. He was far past caring whether anything he said was dangerous, or sensible, or what. All he cared for was to even up for all that Jack had heaped upon him.

He was well started, too. Jack's voice no longer held laughter. "How d'you mean that?" he said, sounding like a threat.

"None of your goddamned business!" Pat yelled back.

"What if I mean to make it my business?" Jack shouted.

"The weather's your business, so you said! Go tend to it!"

A bush beside the trail, its branches stitched heavy in ice, brushed at Pat. Pulling down his head, he thrashed out to ward it off, and when he looked up again, Jack was there, grabbing his coat collar.

"You stinking little ferret!" Jack said.

Pat jerked against Jack's hand. "Let go of me, goddam it!"

"I mean to make it my business!" Jack said.

Under him Pat's horse moved forward. Reaching back, he tried to break Jack's grip, but it was too strong. Then the horse was gone and his free weight wrenched him loose to crash down through the tear and bite of the bush to the litter of rock below the snow cover.

Above him now the sound of Jack's laughter drove all that might have been caution from Pat's head and, rolling up, his hand went down to his knife and jerked it free. Driving up in a lunge, the blade went streaking high for Jack's throat, and seemed almost on the point of going in when there bloomed before his face an orange flower, and a blast of heat and sound cast him backward.

Now he lay in the snow, but he felt no cold. The flower had gone to root in his chest, and flamed in red glory there. Campbell's face appeared to fill the world above him, but now the edges of that world began to blacken, and the face grew smaller. In curling petals, the flower withered, but the space it left was empty, and now the cold did come.

But, for one moment there, he'd known what lay in Jack's thoughts.

CHAPTER TWENTY-TWO

Just inside the fringe of pine, Troy drew up to wait for the others, and in halting a sound reached up that made him turn and look along the trail below him, wondering. It seemed like gunfire, but he wasn't certain; yet even if he couldn't guess what might have happened down there three hundred yards under him, something warned him not to go back to find out.

So he stayed in the trees, and in a moment saw Jack swing down to earth and, after a step, pull down with his pistol on something shapeless in the snow; and the sound came again.

There was no doubt that time. As clear as could be the pistol had been fired, and the shapeless thing was human. Jack had killed McGuire, and now he was starting to pull his clothes apart.

For a moment after that, all of the dark unknowns in Jack Campbell came together in Troy's thoughts and pushed him into panic, and he was fifty yards farther into the trees before he got hold of himself again and stopped his horse. And even then his mind still went charging on in all directions.

"What to do?" it seemed to shout. "What in God's name to do?"

Beyond him the saddle reached upward, grew level in a while, and then fell off into space on the south flank of the range. Should he chance it? Ride on down into Lonesome Valley and on toward home? Home was where he wanted to be now, more than anywhere.

But he knew he'd never get there. Saving a pair of venison ribs that he kept in a pocket to gnaw on as he rode, the food was carried by the pack string. And what was way worse, so were his shotgun and revolver; they'd got so heavy along the snowy trail.

Maybe he should stay right here, and go through motions of making camp—start a fire, and gather windfall wood, to make it look good. The wind had cleared the ground, and the shelter was fair—though the downside would no doubt be better.

But this would do for show; and then when Jack came up and told him what had happened, he could show surprise and complete innocence.

But what if Jack didn't choose to tell him? What if Jack should just ride in and gun him down, too?

Then again, it might be best to turn about and go back down to Jack and his grisly work, and brazen it out. Tell him he'd seen the shooting, and ask him how come? Jack might even tell him. It surely was no secret that a feeling lay between him and Pat; one of long standing, according to remarks of Pat's in the last two days.

But who in his right mind would go unarmed and ask a killer about his handiwork?

That's what Jack was—a killer; and maybe not the first time either, if Pat's hints meant anything.

So there was a hole in that, too, and brought him back full circle to a saddle in the Black Hills, a thousand miles from nowhere, and a killer behind him.

And he *was* in back of him now: an alley in the timber gave out onto the slope below, and a glance down through it showed the pack string's narrow scar in motion again. No doubt Jack was already scanning the trees in search of him.

What to do? What to do?—and his eye ran wildly about in a panic of hunting a way out; any way would do.

Then, all at once, he found it, and he knew what to do. His glance had touched on the points that lifted from the saddle on each side, steep tumbles of massed stone that wore tatters of snow and ice upon their dark shoulders. From below you saw them only by chance, for they were hidden by the roof of pine overhead except in some places.

It was chance that put him under such a place now. And through it, the two points showed themselves, the one to his left nearer. He made his way toward the heave of the bottom, taking care to guide his horse across clear ground, so that its tracks wouldn't show—though they mightn't anyhow in the heavy gloom of dusk. And at the base, stood down and led the way through the brush among the sprawl and stumble of fallen rock, careful again about the snow; but after three or four minutes, seeing that footing could be chosen less by where he *wished* to go than where the horse *could* go.

That meant taking chances on tracks, for the drift and fall of the snow hugged close around those places that were most nearly level. He himself could climb a point to bridge a trough where their passage might be noticed; but the horse couldn't. He also could thread his way along wind-cleared ledges; but the horse couldn't do that either. Moreover, they'd now passed through the early clutter and come to face the raw, steep flanks where headway to the top would be at times a straight climb, hand over hand.

Here, at a point where his eyes came level with the crowns of the trees, he stopped. Above, the rock heaved up, plane on broad plane. Here and there the faces were scarred by shadowy clefts that would bear him farther. But the horse could never reach beyond this place.

What to do now? It was the same old thing again; the same old agony of choice. Yet this time it was at least narrowed down to one of two moves and, to be truthful with himself, it wasn't even that. For nothing on earth could keep him from getting as far away from Jack's reach as he could. He was barely a third of the way up, and there still remained all that lay above him to hide in.

He hated to lose his horse, but the threat to his life was far more real. How could it pay to lose that, in order to keep the animal near?

Likely, Campbell would take it anyway.

Well, he could strip the rigging, at least. Doing so, he stuffed it into a hole that lay handy, then laid the blanket over it to guard against weather. A Navajo, the blanket's blend of earth colors could fool Jack's eye, should he climb this far.

Then, on rolling a few odd stones against the cache, he took the horse by the jawbone and turned it about on the way downward—while the great searching eyes seemed to ask why it should go to meet what he did not dare meet himself. So he slapped its rump hard; and then, to make sure, shied a stone at the lifting heels.

Now he turned and, reaching with both hands, began to work upward. Below him, as he made his way to a ledge and paused to breathe, he heard the horse descending toward the saddle; and he might have looked, to be sure. But he couldn't bring himself to look again. The soft and asking eyes were already too much in his mind. They were like those of a friend that were turned upon him, as he left, in wonder and hurt; and too remindful of that other friend he'd left the same way yesterday.

On the peak, the wind blew; freshening again, perhaps, or perhaps it had blown so all along up here, coming solid and unbroken from the Rim, passing high over lowlands and valleys. Blistered with a lean, raw snow, it snagged upon the heights, humming. Dark cloud, piled a mile deep, it seemed to Troy, choked the full sweep of the sky, and rode the wind's drive to the south.

Huddled into a shattered crag on the highest splinter he could find, no part of the land that he could see was free of snow. And no part of the sky was light of the leaden swell of cloud. It went on and on to the end of his sight and still, no doubt, beyond that. It might even reach as far as home, and at this minute be flooding over the passes and spilling into the Valley.

In his mind's eye, the cracked gray earth and the thirsted wrack of tree took shape. Under the blaze of sun, heat sucked at them.

Then he saw it all as it might be now, the honed edge of drought turned and softened in white and, under the bed of snowfall, the slow melt soaking downward into the earth in even wet.

An ache came into his throat; he pulled his eyes away from the south and looked down. From here, a hundred feet and more above the joined crowns of the pine, he had an eagle's view. As if dropped from the sky to land as it might, the point of rock fell off below him smash upon smash of broken, piled stone until, in broadened spills of rubble, it went from sight among the brush thickets and trees.

Holding to the rock nearby, he leaned outward, trying to see down through the dark roof of trees. Though he'd been up here only five or ten minutes, it was still a long while since he'd seen Jack and the string. The slope under the trees fell off so sharply that their high crowns blocked off a good deal of it to view, even from here.

He ought to be along, however, Troy thought, by now. Maybe Jack had already found his horse, roving about alone without rigging. *That*'d tell him something, and likely send him slinking through the dim trees, searching. Jack knew he wasn't armed, too.

Unless maybe Jack meant to hunt him down in daylight. Dark was now thick and close below the pine, and he might make camp and bide his time. Yet, though Troy stared down until his eyes swam, no tongue of flame licked at the black.

Then all at once a voice reached him, a voice so keening high it seemed made of the wind—if he hadn't known better.

"Troy! You, Troy!"

It joined the wind, then rose over it, sounding clear. Troy pulled back, pressed against the lift of stone behind him.

Not that he'd be seen now with night folding down. But he still remembered Pat sprawled under Jack's fire. And if he bent around the point, he could see Pat yet, a far mark on the white slope.

The cry came again, "Troy—hey, you, Troy!" and after it sounded still a third time a silence drew down for a moment.

Then the silence was broken by three shots run together in rapid-fire. The sound slammed up sudden and sharp against the planes of stone, and Troy pressed back still harder, his heart lifting.

There were only the three, and after their echo passed off, quiet returned to stay. There was still the sough of the wind in his ear—growing some, it seemed—but no more from Jack. At first he felt a sense of relief, the way you feel on breaking free of danger; but as the time of quiet grew longer, he felt uneasy.

What was Jack doing now? he asked himself. At least, when he was noising around down there, his whereabouts were known.

Likely now he was searching. Failing to draw Troy out with his racket, that would be next. He might even have picked this point to start with. The notion scared him badly enough to look down again. Edging forward on his stomach, he poked out his face. Peering down, he half expected to see Jack right under him, his gun muzzle yawning.

But he wasn't there. Nor was there any sign of him in all the wild shatter of stone shapes that fell away to the bottom.

But rather than feel better over this, the fright grew bigger. That Campbell couldn't be found on one side of the point only made it likely that he was climbing another side. He'd hardly show where expected.

Now a kind of frenzy took hold of Troy. What he'd looked on as a hideout had developed into a trap. Lurching up, he started crawling and pulling himself about the top of the point. Under, over and around the stone blocks he went, clawing, creeping, leaning out over nothingness. His knees were torn by the rough granite faces and his hands were made raw from gripping at frost-split cracks; he wallowed in snow pockets and at times slipped on hidden ice that threw him into a teeter of balance so hairline thin that fright galloped through him in white sheets. And that Jack went unseen from all of these places meant only that Troy must move faster, to be back in time to catch him out from cover on the next round.

There was no sure way to know how long this kept on, but a moment arrived at last when he became himself again. All at once he stopped his scrabbling about; leaning on stone for support, while his body shook in weariness, he saw the sky closed down in night altogether. Saving for a thin, still light from the snow, the world had gone dark.

He went to the ledge where he'd hidden before; and for a time lay back from the wind while his breathing grew more even. There was no longer any point in running back and forth on lookout, if there ever had been. He'd never find Jack in the dark, no more than Jack could get sight of him.

Cooler in mind now, he grew angry and disgusted with himself, and it didn't matter that he had no weapons. Let him come, he'd roll rocks onto him, or skin stones. Knowing his ground gave him a chance at least. In any event, he'd have to make his stand and take what came.

But no more chasing around like a squirrel in a cage; a person couldn't carry on like that and call himself a man. That was boy's business, or a coward's.

But he had, a small voice said. And, facing it, he had to admit that he was scared half to death of Campbell and maybe had been all along, since first knowing him. Coming down to it, maybe that stood in the background of his old liking for him, his careful study of Jack's ways, and his trying them out on his own, unseen—except that Ash always seemed to be looking.

If he feared Jack, so did he respect him, for at times the two were brothers. Maybe in being too young to have your own shape, you hunted a shape in others, older maybe, who had a look of having been places and having done things; a look of secret knowing, of power held back against need, maybe of threat held in, but known to be there.

A fellow liked to cotton up to such; and then, all at once, they unwound and laid about them in all directions, and you had to hop fast to get out of the way. If you did so, you got off with a lesson.

But what if you didn't? Where at were you then?

Up on a goddam rock, that's where, half dead from cold and fright, waiting for something to happen, wishing to heaven you'd never let Jack run you, and wishing, too, that things done in bad spirit could be set right again somehow. For all that the words on leaving camp had been his, the thought behind them hadn't been—or hadn't seemed to be; things got so twisted when a fellow let himself be led on.

An hour might have passed now, all told. The wind had grown stronger still, and the fine, hard snow shotgunned all about him. The Verde warmth was wholly gone from the air and the cold drove deep in. It didn't help much any longer to beat himself with his arms. Stranded here all night, he could even die before morning.

He leaned ahead, looking below. All was black now. Dark had bled the shape from rock and tree and bush, and night joined them all. There was still no firelight either; but Jack could yet be there.

But he couldn't last on this rock forever. Going down, he mightn't either, but in the dark he might have a chance. Careful, he might get near enough to Jack to use a rock before he got his pistol going.

Then there was another point—one grown out of the disgust he felt with himself. If a fellow was going to get it, it was better to do so fighting than sit and wait for it. A man would do so, and a person calling himself a man would, too.

Just then, as he choused his thoughts toward starting down, a motion pecked at his sight. It seemed to be down on the trail to the Verde, but was so dim and far on the pale snow that he had to look to the side of it to be sure. And even then, it took another minute.

Then he knew what it was; only a pack string would line out so.

He heard himself laugh. He pulled himself up to see better, and then as the sight made him weak, he had to hang onto the rock. It was Jack. By God, it was! He was pulling out and heading back north.

He was free—and the word stood in his mind. He was still alive and, moreover, his chance to go on living was good. Ten minutes' time would take him to his blanket; five more would see a fire going. With dawn he could head for Prescott.

It was only slowly that he wondered why Jack should head back where he'd come from. Then it came to the center of his thoughts.

Why head north? Why not west or south to fair weather?

Then he knew the answer there, too. No doubt Jack was on a killer's rampage, and meant to wipe out all who knew or might find out. That he had been let be himself, meant only that Jack believed that, unarmed and unhorsed, he'd never leave the country alive.

But it wouldn't be so for Ashley and Julius, unsuspecting and waiting for help. Likely Jack would be taken for that help, and the error would be known too late.

So he guessed he wasn't free, after all. He knew what must be done, but admitting it to himself came slow, for with it dread of Campbell returned. But he knew he had to follow him as best he could and hope to be in time. After all that had happened, he owed that much to Ashley. And for himself, he knew that he could never return to the Valley with tidings of Ashley's death, unless he'd first done all he could to prevent it.

It surprised him that the knowing came so quick, and somehow settled his mind, too.

In ten minutes he had his blanket; the rest could wait until later, if there was one. In ten more he found the tracks of his horse—at the end of the string where Jack had started back down.

So much for that—as he killed the match in the snow and stood up.

Below on the slope, all sign of Jack and the string was gone; he'd be miles ahead now, deep in the folds of the downgrade. At the edge of the trees, where he rigged the blanket round him, he felt the air that came from the Verde —less biting than on the peak and quieter.

But it would all be different tomorrow—when he'd crossed the river and begun to climb the icy, wind-torn benches reaching north. The country could still get him, even if Campbell didn't.

But whether it did or didn't, no longer scared him so, for the longer the storm blew here, the deeper south would it move. Whatever it brought him, it could only bring saving good to home.

That surprised him, too, for at all times before he'd turned from such thoughts. But now, moving out, the hope that it might be so went with him.

CHAPTER TWENTY-THREE

Campbell came down the mountain that night, struck the Verde long before dawn and, fording over, traveled on east to a grove of winterkilled cottonwood trees that marked the point where the creek came into the river.

Here, toward mid-morning, he went into camp to cook breakfast and feed up the horses on cottonwood branches, and to sleep for a couple of hours by his fire.

By noon, he was moving on once more, north now, along the old trail made coming down, lifting onto the snowy benches that led to the Rim and the canyon.

With afternoon half gone, he rode in distant sight of the heave of red monuments: in back of them, the ragged line of the Rim began to form, though not yet telling too much of itself. Soon after, the first of the piñon and juniper and cedar stood squat and alone on their ridges, like sentries at outpost.

It was cold, though not so bad yet as coming down. The wind was less, and the sand-sized snow that riddled him from time to time was only fitful. It was as if the storm was undecided what to do next—maybe thinking to pass on, but in the bulge and roll of dark cloud that drowned the sky, showing a threat of what could happen if it stayed.

Meanwhile, it only sniped and niggled at him.

But Campbell didn't mind it now, nor the threat of worse. He was rigged against cold, and against the storm, too, should it set in again. With food and weapons and blankets for three men, six horses that he could ride or pack as he chose, he was fixed for any weather. What he had here was only an inconvenience; and he could always hole up and sit out a real tail-twister. All he'd need was some cottonwood limbs from time to time to keep the animals going.

And what if they didn't all make it? So what? Losing a couple would lessen his care of them. Two were riding light anyway. Just now he rode one belonging to Troy, and for a moment, as the horses moved in his thoughts, Troy joined them.

It puzzled him yet, what might have happened to him. Standing up in that saddle last evening, no amount of yelling or shooting his pistol had raised him. It was queer. Maybe he'd gone over onto the downslope and lost himself. That was possible. Could be, too, he'd toppled off a ledge somewhere. In the growing dark, that could happen.

But then his horse had come poking up, unrigged, and how could that be explained? You could only guess. Likely, on finding a place to camp, Troy'd stripped the horse and put it on picket. Then, coming back from a search for wood, say, he'd found it drifted and had gone looking. And it was then he'd got lost, or fallen, or whatever.

Of course, you couldn't be sure; all tracks ended where the snow thinned off, at the edge of the trees. Under them was only frozen mulch of old pine needles and, in the dark of the day and the shadowing crowns above, you couldn't tell anything.

So, casting about in the dark for sign was pointless, just as hanging around on top of the mountain was. In view of what he'd taken from Pat, his time could be better spent in other directions.

Too bad for Troy, it was. Campbell could have used him as a witness, too, though it was doubtful that he'd seen. He hadn't been in view anyhow. But he could be told; after all, a man who held out on his *compañeros* in a gold hunt deserved to die. It was self-defense, too. Troy needn't have said more than that, and a cut in the find would have helped him over details that might have raised thorny questions.

But, like Pat, Troy was no doubt way beyond asking questions by now. Just as he knew himself to be beyond returning again to the Valley—a thought that had grown large once more, on finding what Pat had. But descending the mountain alone had ended that for all time. You couldn't face the kinfolk of a man that you'd abandoned, which is how it would be looked on. There was Merril and Julius, too, if they ever got out. They'd have their stories.

So, cut and run then was best. Take the cream of the lode as quick as he could, and leave the country altogether. He'd always done better as a loner anyway.

Night, the second night now, came down from the sky, darkened out from the deep red of rock that flanked the creek, and dimmed the blind white of snow. A stilly night, deep and breathy in cold, but holding back snow and wind, as if waiting, still figuring.

The country kept lifting. With good dark he passed among ridges massed black in piñon and juniper. The heave and tower of monuments seen earlier in the day pressed near, dark flanks rising beyond sight.

Through early evening, he went on north, steady, the pack string at trail. But three or four hours after day ended, he searched out a gravelly ford in the creek and crossed to the far side.

Now turning east and away from the water, he began to swing an arc among the monuments, in order to have them as a shield between him and the old camp when he made his way past it toward the canyon mouth.

At what he took for midnight, he edged along a draw toward a wrack of cottonwood standing in winter death. Here, building up a fire for warmth and coffee, he sat in a bundle of blankets gnawing on deer meat, while the string eased itself and fed on branches readied with an ax.

He allowed no more than half an hour for this, however; then he threw on his saddles and packs and tied down his hitches. Pressing on faster now, he drew the end of his arc back toward the creek, and an hour before dawn came under the Rim where the canyon yawned black to the north.

He was now no more than half a mile above camp; at a point where the castled rock stood away, he could make out the dim shape of the sycamore tree, raising its arms above the lean-to.

But he gave it no more than a glance, and scarce a thought to those inside. Time was in his thoughts; he had to beat daylight or risk a chance of being sighted. Leading into the creek, he kept to the shallows of the icy water for half a mile and better so as to leave no tracks that might be found by Merril when out hunting.

Then, making land on the west bank, he pushed on ahead, through deep snow now, for what he guessed as two miles. A number of bends and headlands in the walls then stood between him and the mouth below.

It was far enough to be safe. He looked around for a place to make camp. Beyond him some, a motte of oak bushed out, dark against the wall, and he led the horses into it, turning them about to flatten the snow.

Done with that, he threw them out on close picket and, with no fire, for the cold air of night still moved down-canyon, rolled in all the blankets he had, and stumbled down to sleep in dead weariness.

When he woke, all had gone queer. At first sunlight seemed to fill his eyes; but then he felt the chill press on his skin, and the brightness became snow that lay over his face. Snowslide? A wildness took hold of him; he flung his arms up, swinging, bucked up onto his knees, then burst out into full light.

It was no slide after all. He'd only been covered while sleeping. Four or five inches of fresh fall lay on the level, and it still came down. Doubtless he'd slept longer than planned, for all that the flakes were big, and the air dense with them.

Piling out, he shook his blankets free and began to rig and load the horses. One, now, was down, Pat's grullo, the fetlocks frozen to the bone, the hoofs and cannons cased in ice beyond motion. Wading up that long stretch of creek, then going into camp so soon after, had done it.

Well, it couldn't be helped, no more than could the horse be helped now. A fire was out—though the air seemed still enough. Nor could he shoot it, sound being queer in canyons. And cutting its throat was too bloody; wolves might scent it and, after feasting, trail him.

So he let it be. While it watched him with its sad eyes asking that it not be left, he made his lines fast and, mounting, led the string down from the trees and turned northward up-canyon.

He knew where he was going now, or thought he knew. It was funny how a thing, if let to cook, would finally piece itself out. Not always, maybe, but with Pat holding the pieces, it was bound to in time. Pat had so little to brag on, so little to make himself feel big, that once he did get onto something he almost burst trying to keep it in.

Likely, Campbell thought now, he might have pieced it out sooner if he hadn't been so graveled at Pat these past weeks. But he'd been blind to it, taking Pat's peculiar shifts in mood as party to their talk of pulling out; showing his pleasure that they were, then turning quarrelsome when they didn't move as soon as he might think they should. And sly, too, as on that gusty, cold day of wood cutting.

That hadn't got by Campbell's notice. Trying to wear him down, that's what it was; all a part of Pat's aim to get out.

But where he'd been wrong—or hadn't thought out all the way—was Pat's reason. In taking it as a show of town-man fret over being stuck in wild country, far from ease and warmth and ready chuck, with winter on the march, he'd missed the true meaning.

But he saw deeper now. Pat had wanted to leave, all right; but only to get them away from what he'd learned of, and then sneak back to this country later on and hog it all to himself.

Well, he deserved what he'd got; and on other scores, too.

Small things adding up, he thought, as he plowed on through the falling snow, leading the string among the rocks and brush of the bottoms, often afoot now.

A box canyon—not too far ahead: that was one. Pat had spoke of an elk seen there, but his hesitation with the word now made it the horse that Julius had lost: another. Then, maybe thinking it a slip, he'd told a wild tale of a bear fight to cover up: still another.

In themselves, they meant nothing, and even together didn't mean much until that rock that Pat had stolen from Julius made sense of them.

And even then you needed Pat's big mouth to give it proper order.

But then you had only to pin down the diggings that Julius had made. Getting out as he had, rigging and tools and gear had likely been left all over the place. Even in this snow he ought to find something.

There would be a hole, too, dug or blasted in the canyon wall. Only hard-rock mining could account for the nugget that Pat had carried.

Beyond a spill of rock that, under the snow, made footing bad, a second horse went down, his own this time. He stripped the pack and split the load among the others, and left it as he had Pat's grullo. Through the snow folding down behind, he heard it neighing, calling out that its leg was broken.

The snow was deeper now, four or five miles and maybe as many hours above where he'd slept; taken with the sharp rise and fall of secret rock underfoot, his pace was way slower than yesterday. He was colder, too; in open country he'd ridden muffled in blankets from stirrup to chin. But here he walked, feeling for hidden dangers under the snow.

Once or twice he'd stumbled into the creek, too, and while he'd dried his boots as best he could, the freeze crept into his feet all the same. Soon enough it grew to be really painful, and every so often he caught himself wanting to halt awhile and build up a fire. But whenever that happened, he put it out of his mind, and pushed ahead harder than ever.

Let them hurt—walking would make the blood move anyhow. Stopping now would only invite him to camp, when he meant to get as near the lode as he could before night. With luck, he might even find the diggings by dark. Thoughts of gold had a heat of their own.

So he kept on moving ahead, not stopping, nor even letting himself think of it, punching on through the snow, the brush and rubble of rock, the lead rope taut; feeling the hurt of cold reaching up his legs, and fighting it back as a thing that could make him quit.

Then, all at once, the wall gave way at his left; poking through the screen of snowfall, his eyes made out the dim break that opened west. A lift came into his chest; no doubt lay in his mind that he should turn here. More than once, while learning the country above, he'd traced its edge a ways; and he knew it traveled west too far for Pat to have gone around the head and chanced on another, farther along. Days would be needed for that.

Now, pulling under the steep and narrow box walls, the feeling that he might be near the diggings made him strive to move faster yet. While there was no way to know till he saw them, things pointed so.

Hadn't Pat found Julius near the mouth of this canyon?

And, busted up, Julius couldn't have traveled far, could he?

He hadn't walked, that was sure; nor ridden, either. And if crawling or afloat, he could only have come a short distance.

So he tried to make time again, as on yesterday; but he soon found himself moving even more slowly than in the main canyon, for now he had wind to fight. Before it had roared overhead, coming from the west and northwest, across the canyon at right angles, and letting down its snow silent and still. But now in this narrow box, the wind had its course to follow at ground level; a wind that in its long, howling run made him lean ahead with all his weight; and at bends and headlands, it backed and grew fluky, so that often he lost his balance and sprawled flat. In the air the snow no longer fell in large, quiet flakes but came slatting and driving into his face, blinding and ice-edged.

But the worst was the cold. He'd always hated cold. Yesterday, swathed in blankets, he hadn't noticed it; and this morning, moving afoot in the big, stilly canyon had at least let him bear it. But here in the yell and screech of the wind, it bit and drove and, like fire, worked to gather him into it.

He hadn't gone past the mouth a mile before he knew he'd made a mistake in trying to reach so far in one day. He ached all over with new cold, and the old cold of his feet and legs had gone still higher. Common sense should have put him into camp at the fork until morning.

For a moment he thought of going back; but in the next he told himself that he was damned if he'd turn loose of ground hard won.

He kept on, lunging and driving ahead on will and main strength, and it brought him on what might have been half a mile; then when his strength was nigh gone, he squeezed another half from pure will alone.

But then he knew he'd reached his limit. His stomach had filled with ice and his legs and feet were nearly altogether numb. Leaning on his horse for support, he heard his breath above the wind, sounding in his chest like a waterfall.

Well, he'd camp here, he told himself while his breathing eased. And having come to that, the comfort and warmth of coffee, of hot food, and a great, roaring blaze, enlarged in his head.

He looked around for wood and at first saw none; then, against the wall, he made out through the streaked air what seemed an old snag blown down from above. All else, and there wasn't much, was buried.

But the snag would do, and he pulled an ax from a pack and, crossing the few yards through the drifts, set to cutting a branch, aiming at the knot where the pitch would be found.

One fell, and after another was down, he pulled his knife to whittle shavings for kindling. But his hands were now too cold to cut a fine slice, and the spindle of flame that he struck with a match wouldn't take well.

He tried again, cutting the shavings still finer; and this time, while the flame sprang into ready life, the wind came scooping down to kill it.

He lit it again, hunching and spreading his coat as a shield; and now the wind, in a strong back eddy, sucked it out.

He tried a fourth time, but the wind was there again, pouncing.

The fifth time, he dropped the sulphur-topped block from which he cut matches; then, having cut and struck the match, dropped that, too. His hands could no longer feel them or hold them right.

Now he was scared. This cold was going to kill him if he didn't soon find shelter for his fire, and he looked wildly around him. Nothing showed at all down below, but as his glance went over the wall above, it chanced on a cut that had the dark look of an opening. Under it, the snow slanted down at an angle that seemed to cover a slope.

It took him over five minutes of gasping work before he felt the stone floor under his knees. From the edge it seemed to be some kind of cave, but as the glare and head-on-driving blast of snow had nearly blinded him, there was nothing beyond but black.

Well, it didn't matter now anyway. What mattered was fire, and he was out of the wind at last. Turning about so as to have daylight, he fought again the battle of shaving kindling, and cutting and striking matches.

Once, as down below, the shavings were too heavy; and once, too, he dropped a match which died before he could pick it up.

But on the third try, he had fire. That time all went well, the flame soared fat and healthy through the shavings and then through bigger pieces. Now he slowly edged in the knot, and when the flames came boiling upward in the hiss and sweet smell of burning pitch, he took it up as a light and, standing, turned around to see where he was.

What struck his eye stunned him. It was still dark, but there was light enough from the smoky torch to bring out of the wall beyond a dazzle and glitter, as of flecks of glass or metal glancing fire. He couldn't get near the meaning at first sight, but when the golden color pressed bright on his mind, he knew what it was.

A shout left him. He dropped the torch and stumbled ahead and pressed his hands on the shimmering surface. He moved them over the dancing marks, and now they shone still brighter, until the whole wall was radiant.

That was when a soft rushing sound touched his ear. Very quickly it grew louder, and when he looked around there was an instant when he saw a lake of flame that ran outward from his torch, leaped through a coil of line, and swallowed now at a rounded bulk.

Gulped up in such speed and fury, the coil behaved like fuse; and the bulk seemed to be marked as a powder keg. But it only stood in his sight, falling short of true meaning. He hadn't the time to grasp it, for now the light swelled and roared and he felt himself drawn into the heat and sound and whiteness of the sun.

And just as it enveloped him, a random, runaway thought streaked in to say that he was warm at long last, and would never again be cold.

CHAPTER TWENTY-FOUR

Coming after what seemed an age of storm and wind and cloud and air blurred and stitched with snow, sunlight and blue sky were strange things to look on again, Ashley thought. Though it had started clearing off a few days back, the deep cold that followed the blow had kept them in the lean-to until yesterday, and he was still unused enough to the change to pause from time to time in putting together the poles and straps of the litter, and look around to make sure it was all true.

But it was true enough. The sun was up there, all right, bright in a clear sky. The cold had lessened more today, too; and all around camp there seemed to be an unbending, as the hard freeze unlocked.

From the lean-to's eaves, icicles, glassy and long and as sharp as bayonets, streamed down their melt in a busy drumming. On top of the roof, a choke of steam rose up from dark patches that looked wider each minute. Now and then a feathery spill of snow came off the sycamore tree. The creek no longer smoked, and it carried upon it now a freight of ice that had loosened and worn away from rock along the banks.

The animals had come alive again, too. All about, sign of rabbit marked the snow, the feathers of their toes leaving delicate marks ahead of each leap; the tracks went every which way. Here a coon had passed by, turned aside to prowl around the lean-to, then gone on to the creek. Deer, too, were abroad, the snow sharply cut in small hearts by their hoofs. Beyond, on the bench, the horses had come now from the shelter of the piñon trees and stood in the flood of sunlight while it worked along with their body heat to melt the snow and ice on their tails and fetlocks. He noted that the calico, for all his travel around the countryside, looked fit enough.

From the easy feel of the air, an unknowing person might take it that spring was here. But, of course, it wasn't. This was only a pause between blows, the end of an early storm, with the main works yet to come.

Still it was a day that augured for a spell of fair weather; and a good enough one on which to start leaving this country for home.

From inside the lean-to, where he was doing up the packs, Troy stuck out his head and blinked in the sunlight.

"How you coming, there, Ash?"

"Pretty near done," Ash said. "I guess it'll hold him all right. Anyhow, let him down easy if it don't."

"I'm about set here," Troy said, starting to crawl out. "I can bring the horses down, if you like."

"Might as well," Ash said. "We'll have to get them rigged ahead of fitting this thing on."

Troy stood now, and looked around, still blinking.

"You reckon it's safe to move?" he asked.

Ashley didn't miss that Troy seemed more inclined now to ask about things, rather than tell. Any other time before showing up here back at camp, it would have humbled him. But some changes had come over him. It was just as well not to notice too much, however.

"Not altogether maybe," he said. "But I doubt we'll get a better chance until spring."

"No, I'd say the same," Troy said. "We ought to get four, five days anyhow, before the next. That'll see us into Prescott, at least. Prescott sound all right to you?"

Troy frowned at the snow and hitched at his pants. He was still getting used to his different self, with the going awkward at times.

"The best, I'd say," Ash answered. "Take it in easy stages. Moreover, we ain't hiding from anyone any more. Be a chance to get Julius some proper care, too."

"Not that you ain't done well by him," Troy said.

You learn from fixing calves, Ash almost said, but didn't. Troy's face had reddened like coals.

"Well, I'd best bring 'em in," he added, and started off.

Ashley watched him make his way along the bench through the snow, limping some; and there came to his mind for a moment the sight of Troy five evenings back, when he'd ridden out of the freshening gale like a ghost, streaming a tatter of saddle blanket, and falling half off the calico's back while he kept on shouting, "Look out for Campbell! 'Ware for Campbell!" and not quitting till Ash had made it plain that Campbell wasn't about, and hadn't been.

He'd been lucky, all right, Ash thought now, watching him among the horses. Lucky to find the calico down by the Verde, and lucky to make it back here with just a foot frozen. Without the horse he mightn't have made it at all, once the blow had begun again. And only time would tell if he'd keep all the toes on that foot; they'd shed plenty of skin already.

Just to think of Troy's journey made Ashley shiver, and he knew he'd heard only a part of it, too. What remained, if it ever came out, would take time. Being the part that had to do with how he acted now, it was still locked up in him.

But it suited Ashley if he cared to keep it there.

But now Troy was coming down the bench, the picket ropes in hand, and now the horses were at the lean-to, and now the rigging was going on. The packs were brought out and tied down on the one horse left for such use. The other two were saddled, and would also carry the litter.

"We're surely thinned out in stock," Ash remarked when the hitches were thrown and tied down.

"Uh-huh," Troy said. "Having that pair of mine that Campbell took would make us look better. It beats me where he got to. I lost all sign of him down below somewhere."

"Could be fifty miles off now," Ash said. "More, given he traveled. He was fixed for it, as you said."

"Yes, he could be. Funny how I figured he was heading here, though. Everything seemed to point to it."

"Well, I'm glad he didn't," Ash said. "No doubt Pat filled him up on killing. I'd be surprised if we saw him again."

"He won't dare to show himself around home anyhow," Troy said.

"No, he's on the dodge now," and Ashley raised the end of the litter that was now ready. Reaching, Troy took up the other, and they slid them into the stirrup leathers of the standing horses.

"Damn thief," Troy said. "In some ways a thief is worse than a killer, it seems to me."

Then, as Ash began to tie the thongs run through the holes drilled into the end of the poles with a heated awl, Troy said—as if the thought had spread out more—"Not that I mean to make a lot over that pair; I ain't forgetting that you lost a burro and dog, Ash."

Ashley paid strict attention to the thongs. "It's all right," he said. "I don't guess either could be helped."

"I meant to speak of it before now," Troy said. "I can't explain why I didn't, though I ain't excusin' myself. No guts, I guess. I wasn't my own man."

"It's all right," Ash said again. Troy could hardly have said it better. It was more important to have him as he now was than to dig up the cause of old hurts and worry them.

Then the thongs were tied, and the litter resting level and stout. There seemed no more to be done now, excepting to load up Julius and pack him with blankets against the journey. Casting his eye about, Ashley saw the woodpile almost level with the ground now. The tarp that covered the entry of the lean-to would be left; it was still too stiff with freeze and ice for folding. Under the snow there might be found a picket pin or two; but he didn't think so. One way or another, all had been accounted for.

"It sure doesn't look like much, does it?" Troy said in a moment.

It was what Ash was thinking. Already it looked abandoned and dead, a place without any meaning or purpose. But it had been a good-looking camp at one time, when hopes still ran high.

"I guess it didn't come to much either," Troy went on. "Everything, I mean; all told, it was a loss."

Ashley nodded, but on second thought wasn't so certain. It looked so on the face of it, but underneath there seemed to be things that went against it. It was true he'd lost most everything he'd brought; but he'd been able to make himself face that loss. That was something maybe. There was Lilly, too, and how he looked on her now, as against an earlier time. Hadn't it been for all this, it might have been a long while in coming; maybe too long.

Maybe bigger, though, in its way, was that he felt more sure of himself now. All that the country here had laid upon him, he'd got out from under. It hadn't borne him down, in body or heart or mind, either one—as it might have done, and had tried more than once. He'd survived, you might say, and felt himself added to by having done so.

But he could hardly make that clear to Troy; it wasn't altogether clear to himself. But he remembered something else then.

"Don't forget our dust," he said. "There's still that. It'll hit pretty near three hundred dollars altogether."

"That's so," Troy said. "Still, it ain't a whole lot."

"A hundred dollars apiece about, with the split as it now is."

"It's bigger than it was, all right. Pay for my horses anyhow, and some left over. But it's sure thinner than what we figured on."

"It was just figuring, though," Ash said. "We never really had it."

"Uh-huh," Troy said, thinking. Then he laughed. "Speaking of Campbell—for a wrong man, he was sure right about one thing: Julius."

Ashley nodded there, too, but again he wasn't so sure. Not that Julius hadn't convinced him of his rare state of mind. But Julius had one time made a remark that had stuck in Ashley's head ever since; it related to the grass back home in the Valley, what they'd spoken of one night in camp below the Bradshaws.

"Last year," Ash said, "Walter Vail bought a Durham bull from Dan Murphey for a hundred dollars."

For a moment, Troy looked blank. Then he got through to what Ashley was thinking of. "Up toward the Arivaipa, wasn't it?" He nodded his own answer. "A pretty big order, though. Slow business, building up a breeding herd. You'd have to sell your pa, too."

"It don't matter if it's slow," Ash said. "You got to start some-where." Nor did Pa worry him any longer. Having hung on in his own way, he felt he better understood Pa's words on that score, and on keeping going until things bettered. It wouldn't surprise him any if Pa should favor the idea.

But that was all in time to come; right now they'd better get out of here.

"We'd best get moving," he said, "if we hope to make much by dark."

"All right, let's roll," Troy said. "Julius now, I expect."

"Watch him," Ash said, pulling back the tarp. "His bite's as bad as his bark now."

"I learned. He nigh forked me last night."

But Julius didn't seem in a biting mood today. He lay on his bedroll, wary and up to the brim with suspicion over the doings, but quiet. By stages they eased him outside and tied him down on the litter.

Only then did he speak. "What's all this? What you doin' to me now?"—as if they'd been tormenting him without end.

"It's so you don't fall out," Troy said. "We're going for a ride. Toppling out onto your head, you might get visions."

But Julius was already off on another trail. "Which of you damned robbers has it?" he said.

"No one's got it," Ashley said, mounting. It was always the same with that question. You were no sooner hooked, than Julius wouldn't say what he was after. Ash wouldn't step in that trap any more.

Looking back now, he saw that Troy was up, too, and settled; he bobbed his head, and they started moving out, but slowly, while they saw how the litter rode. After fifty or seventy-five yards it was coming along well enough to let them move a little faster.

Still it wasn't the pace they could make without it.

"I doubt we'll get too far today, after all," Ash turned and said.

"It don't matter," Troy said. "Just so we're home for Christmas."

That was when Julius spoke again; roused was more like it. "What d'you mean—home? Which way we goin', anyhow?"

"South," Ash told him. "South for home; the San Pedro."

"South?" Julius said in half a shout. "That ain't the way to the gold! The gold is north!"

A hoot came from Troy. "The gold is right here," he said. "You got a hundred dollars in placer dust comin' to you."

Julius loosed a yell. "A hundred dollars! Why, you simple fools, I got a million up there! Stuck away in a cliff, just waiting!"

"So's winter waiting," Ash said. "That's why we're moving out now. Rest easy, hear? Your gold is safe."

But he might better have tried to reason with a stump. If it hadn't been for the ropes, Old Man Harper would have left the litter.

"Turn back!" he yelled. "Goddam it, turn and go back! I'll split with you—make it even three ways!" He beat his hands on the sides of the litter and thrashed against the ties. His voice rose still higher, running into a screeching, "Take me back! Take me back! It's there, I swear it is! It's there, just waiting! I seen it!"

"You know," Troy said, when Julius shuddered down to breathe, "he's sure got faith. Makes you wonder a little don't it?"

"I ain't forgot what happened the last time we wondered," Ash said.

"Me neither. We ain't so dumb as we look any longer." Troy thought a moment, then said, "What we going to do about him once we reach home? Be a long while before he's much good for anything."

"Maybe best to take him into Huachuca. They know him there; off and on, he's peddled beef at the commissary. I expect they'll know what to do with him."

Then Julius broke out again, pure raving now; and after a minute or two, Troy said, "You think we ought to put a stop to that? I never heard a man make such a noise."

Ashley didn't answer right away. His mind had ranged on, reaching toward home and Lilly and Christmas and his folks. He ought to get her something, he thought; something nice, that would show her what his true feelings were. He'd get them all something, now that he had money to spend; he'd never had it before.

Then Troy spoke again, and that time reached him.

"It don't do no harm," Ashley said. "Let him get rid of it. He'll likely run down soon enough."

But Julius kept on yelling for a long time—while the white-breasted countryside swelled and heaved and fell away, while the soaring monuments stood silent red guard around them, while muleys watched from green piñon mottes, and far away to the south, the Black Hills raised snowy shoulders to the shining day.

He went on and on, for a good deal longer than you'd think a man so poor in mind and body could.